Lady Jean

Noel Virtue

Lady Jean

PETER OWEN
London and Chester Springs

PETER OWEN PUBLISHERS
73 Kenway Road, London SW5 0RE

Peter Owen books are distributed in the USA by
Dufour Editions Inc., Chester Springs, PA 19425-0007

First published in Great Britain 2001
© Noel Virtue 2001

ISBN 0 7206 1133 4

A catalogue record for this book is available from
the British Library

Printed and bound in Great Britain by
MPG Books Ltd, Bodmin, Cornwall

For Michael John Yeomans and Miss Bessie Todd.
Love immeasurable.

The author would like to acknowledge and thank
Creative New Zealand for a writer's grant
and the real Mrs Meiklejohn, who inadvertently
provided inspiration.

ONE

She had discovered Henry lying dead on the stairs, just after dawn. His body was stiff and quite cold. She had never loved Henry as much as she'd loved the rest of the family. He had not been an affectionate cat.

Jean sat slumped in the oldest armchair of the morning-room. It was a Wednesday morning, just past eight o'clock. She was listening with headphones to a collection of her blues standards, just reissued under a new label. The french windows were wide open. Through them, along with the unseasonable warmth of an early spring day, came a view of Mrs Meiklejohn. Somewhere beyond sixty and as tough as a major in some territorial army, Mrs Meiklejohn was staring through a gap in the garden wall at a half-empty bottle of Tanqueray standing upright on Jean's lawn. Her concentration was so intense that it appeared she might be attempting to read the label, or perhaps using her mind to levitate the bottle out of sight.

Gleaning and sharing as little information as possible from and with the neighbours without appearing to be rude or churlish, several generations of the Barries had lived in the house on Acacia Road. In decades long gone George Eliot had held her Sunday receptions close by, at least within walking distance. Elizabeth Anne Howard, eventually to be made the Comtesse Beauregard, had lived on Circus Road. The local church on the high street was originally built on a plague pit. In 1823 a murderer going by the name of Morland was buried outside at the crossroads, a stake driven through his stomach.

Jean Barrie had never held Sunday receptions nor been found guilty of any crime, except perhaps for her attempts to eradicate the functions of her liver by drinking too much. It used to be claimed, probably by a good Christian, that gin was a mother's ruin.

Mrs Meiklejohn, taking one long embittered glare towards the open french windows, withdrew. Minutes later Jean heard the slam of Mrs Meiklejohn's kitchen door. She continued to sip at her coffee until the mug, decorated with a William Morris design and chipped, was empty. She reached across to set the mug down on the table beside the chair and picked up her appointment book. *Twelve thirty, lunch with Freida. Must telephone Aunt Dizzy. Anthony Hibbert calling at seven. Dinner?* In a careful hand, with the attached pen, she added, *Bury the cat.*

The house that Jean owns, had been born in and brought up in stands only a couple of hundred yards from the tube station in St John's Wood. Jean had once known but long forgotten when the house had been built and the vaguely distinguished names who previously owned it or visited. It is an ancient house that has survived by careful change of ownership yet only occasional renovation. The hallways and the stairs, like many of the rooms, are permanently in shadow from the dark-stained oak panels and ceiling beams and general neglect. It is not a distinguished house in itself. It is now far less occupied by people than in any time in its long history. Fronted by a low privet hedge that is as neglected as the rooms indoors, there are two concrete tubs on either side of the cracked entrance steps in which red geraniums struggle to impress.

There are two reception rooms leading off the main downstairs hall of the house. The one to the left is used to store box after box of long-playing records, vinyl treasures, now defunct, that Jean has never had the inclination to sell. Billie Holiday, Sophie Tucker, Annette Hanshaw, Helen Morgan, Elsie Carlyle. The boxes sit one on top of the other like a mausoleum to lost vocal fame. The other reception room is an escape for visitors, as it once was for family, to seek solitude in or solace or simple sloth. Overburdened with books and videos on shelves and a small television with in-built video player, the room is dominated by dust and not unpleasant odours from at least the past fifty years and a huge horse-hair sofa sagging with cushions and rugs. Christopher, Jean's erstwhile young man of gardening and culinary and lack of communication skills, is never allowed into the room to clean.

The downstairs hallway, walls festooned with oil paintings and faded pastels and the occasional framed poster, leads directly to the morning-room, the kitchen door also there to the right. The main staircase, which had been cleverly hidden when built, designed by someone wholly undistinguished and forgotten, is in a corner of the morning-room, hidden also from sight with a set of free-standing panels that reach from the bottom stair to the hall door. Upstairs, the drawing-room, vast, formal and unrenovated for decades, was named by a now dead, theatrical relative as the Green Room. It quietly possesses almost the entire first floor. From there stretches a short, dark hallway with doors leading into bedrooms and two *en suite* bathrooms with separate spartan toilets. Another staircase ascends to a self-contained studio flat, where once sat cupboards for the servants and where now lives the long-term lodger known as the Fallen Nun. And on top of the house sits the roof, tiled, angled, where pigeons and starlings and sparrows deposit their bodily waste. When rain falls heavily the roof leaks pigeon- and starling- and sparrow-tainted water down the walls of the uppermost rooms, causing the Fallen Nun to complain with notes that Jean successfully manages to ignore.

'Is that you, Aunt Dizzy? It's your niece. It's Jean.'

Jean explained and enunciated slowly whenever she telephoned her aunt. Elizabeth Barrie was suspicious of being telephoned, having once been traumatized by a series of obscene calls back in the 1970s when an illegal telephone sex-line was created and the number widely misprinted as Aunt Dizzy's own. Jean did not often enjoy the dutiful, twice-weekly calls. Aunt Dizzy still believed that one should shout into the receiver, which, she claimed, helped the electronic voice to speed down the line.

'Is that you, Jean? How lovely of you to call. So unexpected. Just a minute. I've something on the boil.'

Something on the boil was a ruse to help Aunt Dizzy catch her breath. The telephone's shrill bell, never adjusted, caused her, she said, to have heart palpitations which were not healthy for a fragile lady of eighty-one.

'There,' she continued, seconds later, shouting, 'all set. How are you, Jean? Did you hear yourself on Radio Two yesterday? Around four thirty. Or was it the day before? You never sound any different, ducks, even if the programme was five years old. You are an absolute ruddy fool, don't you know? It's time you took yourself in hand. All this retirement business. It isn't healthy. Despite all you went through.'

Jean did not respond. She silently counted to ten.

'Now don't you hang up on me, ducky,' Aunt Dizzy muttered. 'I know you.'

'Would you like to come and stay for a few nights, Auntie?' Jean asked. 'It's been a while. I've bought some of those lamb chops you love, from the food hall.'

'What?'

'Lamb chops! From the food hall in Selfridges. You remember, you couldn't stop exclaiming over them last time you were here.'

'*Couldn't* I?'

There was silence for a moment. Jean heard Aunt Dizzy swearing, her hand over the receiver ineffectually stifling the curse.

'I'm so sorry, ducky, I've these awful medicinal stockings. They're cutting off my circulation and making me irritable. I don't even need them. Bloody doctors. Yes, I would love to come over. How is Freida?'

'Fine. She's fine. Auntie, Henry died last night. Didn't even wake me up.'

'Freida? Freida has *died*?'

'No, Auntie, Henry. Henry died. I found him on the stairs this morning.'

'*Did* you? Well, I am so sorry, ducks. I expect they all die eventually. Cats are only animals, after all. So Freida hasn't died?'

Jean sighed.

'No, Auntie. I'm having lunch with her today. I'll pass on your love.'

'A liquid lunch I expect,' Aunt Dizzy muttered as if to herself. 'When do you want me on board? Shall I order a taxi? I can if you're giving a few days' notice.'

'How about the weekend? Now don't worry, I'll come and collect you in the motor as usual. Just pack a few necessities. Nothing else to bring. You need the change of air. It always does you good.'

'*Does* it?'

Aunt Dizzy Barrie – Elizabeth – also named Doo Lally Barrie by Freida, was Jean's late father's only sister. She had had a checkered life. Threatened with a pre-frontal leucotomy on several occasions throughout her youth for outrageous behaviour with older men and younger women, she had created scandal and unrest within the family. She had never married. She had a son living in California who made action films for television and was reputedly addicted to cocaine. Elizabeth Barrie was so rich she was forever being plagued by charities, whose frequent, money-seeking receptions she attended with religious zeal. Accompanied by 'a young man' of seventy, she referred to him as the One Who Got Away, her only paramour, despite the generally known fact that he was homosexual. Jean had her to stay at irregular intervals, usually over a weekend, when friends occasionally called in without prior arrangement. Aunt Dizzy entertained them with the zest of unbridled youth. Everyone who knew her admired her. She had given up alcohol and aerobics on her seventy-ninth birthday but still occasionally smoked miniature cigars that were handmade for her by an old firm of tobacconists in Manchester. She lived in Mayfair, in a suite of rooms at the top of a hotel and was waited on diligently by the staff. The arrangement suited her, after selling her Hampstead home once a serious fall threatened problems that never ensued and a flat refusal to be placed in a nursing home caused a family crisis.

Jean had spent the previous evening sitting on a blanket on the lawn, clad in only a dressing-gown and thick socks, loud music – not her own – blaring from the morning-room as she sipped straight gin from a fluted champagne glass. She had lain back at one stage, opening the dressing-gown to expose her skin to the night sky, remembering her mother as a young woman dancing naked under the moon, forgetting that Mrs Meiklejohn would be able to see her from her upstairs windows and would more than likely be spying. She had moved indoors eventually, leaving the Tanqueray bottle and going straight to bed, lying there in her vast room listening to the Fallen Nun reciting poetry somewhere up above. The voice had been faint and strangely comforting. It had lulled her into sleep without any warning. If Henry had indeed called to her as he lay dying on the stairs, Jean had not heard.

Now, having attended to the dutiful call to Aunt Dizzy, who would forget about the invitation to come to stay by lunchtime, Jean picked up the box in the hall in which she had placed Henry's body wrapped up to the neck in an old silk scarf. She carried the box through into the kitchen, lowering it down gently on to the side-table by the door. For a few minutes she gazed at the silk-wrapped corpse and cried a little. Henry had been thirteen years old. He had come from a long line of demanding feline companions going back to before her childhood. When Jean was born there had been a fifteen-year-old Henry living at Acacia Road. There had always been a Henry at Acacia Road. Sometimes several at once.

She telephoned Christopher from the hall and asked him to come over, explaining why.

'I have to go out,' she added. 'Lunch. I've left Henry in the kitchen, in a box. Make certain you mark the grave.'

She had never exactly warmed to Christopher. At seventeen he still lived with his parents at Eamont Court, a large square block of unfashionable private flats near the park. Studying law and economics, which he hated, he walked local dogs, tended gardens and generally accepted any task that helped pay his way. He never refused her a visit and came officially on Fridays to clean, attend to the garden and occasionally prepare meals which he left in foil for her to freeze. She usually forgot. Lately his behaviour had begun to change. She sent him a fortnightly cheque or left it on the hall table. Christopher was exceedingly tall with lank black hair and rubbery lips similar to those of a chimpanzee. They were the largest, most peculiar lips Jean had ever seen on a male face. They were always bright pink and compared badly to his sallow, unhealthy skin. Acne scars, a weak chin, combined with a body odour that never ceased to disturb her, made his close proximity uncomfortable. They communicated by note, the telephone and messages taken by his mother, a devout fundamentalist Christian who sent e-mails of complaint and disapproval to the Pope and spoke to Jean over the telephone as if she had filled her mouth with carpet tacks. According to Christopher, his mother had suffered for years from mouth problems over which three GPs and a Harley Street specialist were stumped.

Jean met Freida at a small, familiar and reliable Indian restaurant just off Kentish Town Road, to where they both travelled by minicab, therefore allowing them to drink excessively.

'You're late, Lady,' Frieda complained as soon as Jean appeared but had not even sat down.

'Shut up, trollop, and order me a double.' Jean leant over and kissed Freida on the cheek. Freida had once claimed that this represented the latent lesbian tendencies Jean had never come to terms with.

Freida Weinreb's origins were the result of a casual coupling between a New York press agent and a minor British film starlet. The latter lived alone, ageing badly, somewhere in Yorkshire, breeding Siamese cats and denying Freida's existence. Freida's parents had been married only long enough to have had enough sex to beget her, Frieda was fond of explaining to total strangers, while weeping with intense enjoyment. Unlike herself, who stayed married only long enough to realize the true horrors of a man's sexual organs. She had never been forced to enter a career and join a publisher or a PR company. Money from her daddy, who did recognize her existence, arrived into her bank account from America with a regular smooth flow, and she spent it as easily. Though she had once written a play about female angst that premièred at the Hampstead before it sank gracefully into the pit.

'How's Doo Lally?' she asked, once Jean was settled and the drinks had arrived. Jean smiled. The two never failed to ask about each other.

'I spoke to her this morning. Invited her over for the weekend. Now you must promise to pop in. Come for Sunday lunch. You know she never truly enjoys her visits if you fail to make an appearance.'

'And?'

'What?' Jean was staring at a silver-haired man in a blue flannel suit. He had a cleft chin.

'Did you get a *report*?'

Jean, having hated herself at the time, had arranged for someone to monitor Aunt Dizzy's behaviour at the hotel closely, as there had been veiled complaint. In the guise of a hotel employee, the man was some behavioural assessor who had been recommended to her. He charged a ridiculous fee. Jean nodded. The second round of drinks arrived. The waiter was new. He was wearing pale lipstick. One of his eyelids had been pierced with a minuscule silver disc. Freida glanced up and winced.

'She's been hanging her rinsed undies out the windows of her rooms pegged to a length of rope,' Jean responded once the waiter had moved away. She thought he had winked at her then realized the young man was in certain discomfort with his eyes. It was the age of piercing. Frieda had a small solid silver chain attached across her stomach. According to her, most of her female lovers apparently enjoyed holding it in their teeth during sex.

'So that's not so awful. A little tacky for Mayfair. Or perhaps not.'

'She'd dyed them bright red. The dye dripped down on to some woman's hair and suit as she stood chatting to her husband on the steps below. The woman's threatened to sue. American, of course.'

'Anything else?'

'Someone found her wandering through the foyer at four thirty in the morning, half naked. She claimed she was looking for her maid to get her dressed. She was carrying her handbag and wore little else except those hideous six-inch heels you so stupidly gave her. When one of the female staff took her arm to lead her back upstairs she created a terrible scene.'

'*Did* she?' Freida said with a smirk, imitating Aunt Dizzy's voice. Jean smiled thinly. She glanced across at the cleft chin two tables away. The man had turned to look about him and was discreetly picking his teeth with a fingernail while speaking into a mobile phone. He had close-set eyes. Jean immediately went right off him.

They discussed seriously what could be done. The hotel management were being intolerant, as far as Freida was concerned. They charged a small fortune for Aunt Dizzy to be in residence. Yet it was obvious that professional help was soon to be needed. A nurse. Some full-time companion. A transfer to a home, a possibility they each knew that Elizabeth Barrie loathed and feared.

16

'Of course you could install her at Acacia Road,' Freida suggested. 'Get rid of the Nun. It's time *she* moved out.'

'Aunt Dizzy could never manage those stairs!'

'A stair-lift, then. Some of them take wheelchairs. She might need one. Like in that movie, oh, what was it called? Old. Black and white. *Naked Edge*? Gary Cooper. Some unknown actress used the chair.'

'Her head fell off and rolled,' Jean added.

Freida laughed. They ordered steak and fresh oysters, ignoring the Indian cuisine. They shared an appetite for food which did not appear to have any effect on their weight. They were both thin. Freida claimed that in her case it was from a surfeit of sex. Jean knew she was lying. They were both prone to stress.

'With cleft chins in mind,' Freida suddenly said after their meals had arrived, 'I've some dark news.' She had glanced across at the man Jean had been staring at.

Jean sniffed the oysters. She didn't look up.

'I've seen Wee Willy Winky.'

Jean froze. She raised her sight and not quite looking Freida in the eye said, 'Oh?' and a shiver of something ran down through her. Not fear, not even apprehension. She began to lose her appetite.

'At the Garrick. A new Hare play. Awful, dreadful play. No, I lie. I couldn't understand it. Noticed Wee Willy at the interval. Nice suit, good cut. One minor celebrity blonde slut on his arm, trying to pretend she was his beloved by smiling up at him with gargantuan mouth and teeth like a mule's.'

Jean slid the polished prongs of her fork into an oyster shell and, painstakingly, teased the oyster out.

'Did you speak to him?' she asked after a pause. She stared down at the oyster, then placed her fork back down on to the plate.

'Of course not! We left just after that. Sat in a wine bar. Couldn't have sat through the rest of the play. It's had a sickening rave in the *Mail on Sunday*. Mandy entertained me by relating every sordid detail of her abused childhood.'

Jean continued to stare down at her plate. For a second she could have sworn that one of the oysters moved. She pushed the plate away and took a large swallow of her drink. The restaurant, which was full, suddenly seemed to become hushed. The only sound came from the ice cubes rattling in Freida's glass.

'We both knew His Private Smallness would come back one day, Jean. He may even get in touch. He might be curious as to how you've fared. Hate doesn't last. Not always.'

Jean looked up.

'Who on earth is Mandy?' she asked.

TWO

There is a framed poster that hangs in the downstairs hall at
Acacia Road. It is a badly rendered head-and-shoulders drawing
of Jean standing at a mock-ancient microphone, wearing a gar-
denia in her hair and looking as if she has overdosed on valium.
The poster was created to promote Jean's second collection
of songs, *The Barrie Blues*. She'd hated the title. She had still
been married to William. Back then she was compared to Billie
Holiday and Nina Simone, before she became known as Lady
Jean. The record company were patronizing until she started to
make them a lot of money. For years Jean has hated the poster,
but it was a gift from Freida, so it remains on the wall gathering
dust. The glass is cracked in three places. William, eventually
trapped inside grief, had taken it down one night and thrown it
out into the street.

It was the following day. Jean was sleeping late. Anthony Hibbert had not left until gone midnight. He sat opposite her in
the morning-room collating sheets of handwritten notes Jean
occasionally produced, recollections of her career and early life.
There had once been talk of Jean writing a memoir or possibly a
full autobiography. Since that had never happened Anthony
Hibbert was sent along from the now less enthusiastic publisher
with hope that he might write the book on her behalf, despite
Jean's insistence that, in the event, his name should not appear
on the cover or anywhere inside the book. Freida had tele-

phoned twice during the time Anthony Hibbert was there. She had once informed him in front of a roomful of people that she may well have been a lesbian all her life but he was the only man she had ever craved.

'I am being pressured,' Anthony Hibbert confessed to Jean over dinner. 'There is hope that you might finish your notes by the end of summer. Along with the tapes of course.'

Several conversations had been recorded, though they were a rare event and brief. Jean had lost interest in the entire idea, even of a ghost-written memoir, several months before. She kept encouraging Anthony Hibbert to call, as she enjoyed sharing dinner with him and he had a cleft chin. He was young. He was married to a presenter on the BBC World Service who was, according to Freida, reputed to be a temperamental cow. Jean was also mildly curious as to why Freida found the man so attractive. She didn't. Jean liked him. She admired his easy manner along with his slow, genuine smile. A sad smile, revealing more than he realized. There was a delicacy about him. He created in Jean a maternal longing that she thought had been ended back when life became poisoned by guilt and her own grief.

The house is hushed and seemingly empty now. Perhaps it is asleep. Jean is still asleep upstairs in her silk-sheeted bed. The Fallen Nun, whose real name is Catherine Truman, might be asleep or out. Someone presses the front door bell, then waits but soon goes away. On the roof two collared doves are bowing to each other and gently courting with melodic voices. The house sits solidly beneath the early morning spring sunshine. A stair creaks, then another. The giant Italian-made refrigerator in the kitchen switches itself on with a pleasant hum. A tall, ungainly young man with pale skin lets himself in the back door with a key he keeps around his neck on a length of black cord. He has two moles on his neck and several spots, at which he scratches numerous times a day. He has already checked the newly dug grave in the garden, wherein now lies Henry the Fifth, just to ascertain that nothing has been disturbed. He has brought with him half-a-dozen large, brown, free-range eggs and slices of expensive bacon wrapped in several layers of thick white paper. The paper is soaked through with bacon fat, some of which has rubbed off on to his jacket.

Christopher creeps about the kitchen. His height gives a slight impression that the room's furniture is not suited to it. He is over six feet tall. While the eggs and bacon are spitting satisfactorily in the large, ancient, heavy frying-pan he wipes down surfaces. He empties the small plastic-lined rubbish bin that Jean once threw at William, bruising his left shoulder. Christopher washes a few dishes. He carefully arranges the eggs and bacon on a plain white, chipped porcelain plate before sitting down and eating slowly, gazing about the kitchen and angling his head to listen for sounds from above. When a wracking cough intrudes into the quiet he swiftly gets up out of the chair and rinses the empty plate in the sink. When Jean eventually enters the grubby unmodernized room, still in her nightclothes and yawning, Christopher is busy again at the frying-pan. There is no sign that he has had a meal. The floor tiles are cold beneath Jean's bare feet.

'Two eggs, two rashers of bacon. I'll make coffee,' Christopher says, barely glancing in Jean's direction. Jean does not reply. She turns to leave, now she has entered and let herself be seen. There is a scratching sound inside one of the walls.

'Rats,' Jean mutters. She closes the kitchen door behind her. As the door sticks, she slams it. William had once slammed the door on her and it has stuck ever since as there was damage to the hinges that has never been fixed. She is fully awake now, knowing that Christopher will bring her breakfast on a tray to the morning-room. As she moves into it, the room seems to fold itself around her, like a spacious coffin. She steps across to the french windows and opens them wide. There is a sound like a sigh. Jean sits in her favourite chair. The pair of collared doves that were courting on the roof have now flown down into the garden. Jean has her eyes tightly closed. There is a creaking sound behind her to which she doesn't react. The Fallen Nun appears at the foot of the stairs and glides by, moving silently down the hall to the front door. In the kitchen Christopher swears. He has burnt his left thumb on the frying-pan.

By lunchtime Jean had dressed herself after a tepid bath and the ritual of makeup and brushing her hair. She sat in front of her dresser mirror for a considerable time, gazing at her reflection and examining the lines on her face, trying to decide if new ones had been added during the night. She tried not to let the thought of her being alone in the house deflect from the knowledge that spring had arrived. Summer was up ahead. There was no pressure for her to do anything she did not choose to do. She had grown accustomed to living alone. Though she did not enjoy it, there were compensations: sloth, drinking without being lectured, not having to look her best, not being reminded. And she was not entirely alone. There was Freida, Aunt Dizzy, Anthony Hibbert and others, including the never welcomed but tolerated and useful Christopher Harcourt. More and more over the past few weeks he had begun to appear on days other than the one she paid him for. Preparing breakfast for her was a new development. He had not asked if she wanted a cooked breakfast. He just turned up one morning and kept on doing so. Sometimes breakfast would be a freshly made fruit salad and perfectly browned toast or croissants, warm from the oven and dripping with Swiss butter. It did not appear to concern him that Jean might be dieting. It did not concern her that he also made breakfast for himself. She had noticed.

'Rock melon, strawberries, a dash of lemon juice and fresh pear,' he would say. 'I'll make coffee.'

Where he managed to find such fruits, even out of season, was something she had never bothered to comment on. She did wonder if he had developed a crush on her or, more realistically, had come to regard her as a mother figure. Most of the time she accepted him being there as she did the furniture.

The telephone rang as she sat thinking lazily of her greying hair and an invitation to lunch at her publishers.

'Is that you, Jean?' shouted the familiar voice. 'It's Elizabeth. Your aunt. Am I disturbing you?'

'Only if you want to,' Jean responded.

'What?'

'How are you, Aunt Dizzy?'

There was a pause, a catch of breath and a loud sniff.

'Did you invite me over? I can't remember if it was you or someone else. Shall I order a taxi?'

'You're coming for the weekend, Auntie, don't you recall? I'll collect you tomorrow in the motor. Around noon, if you want. I suggested it yesterday.'

'*Did* you?'

'Are you all right? You sound a little low.'

'I'm fed up. I went downstairs to dine yesterday evening in the Silver Platter but was told I had to have the meal in my rooms and they'd send it all up. I spent over an hour getting ready. You'd think they'd be more accommodating, wouldn't you, Jean, the rent I pay?'

'Well, you did cause that scene, Auntie. In the foyer. Perhaps if you –'

'*Did* I? I don't remember telling you . . . I don't recall any scene. You've mixed me up with one of your chums. How's Freida? I am sure I heard that she'd *died*. Is that true?' There was a split-second pause, then she added, 'Somebody died.'

Ten minutes after Aunt Dizzy hung up, the telephone rang again. It was the manager of the hotel. Quietly, in a calm, too-ingratiatingly servile voice, he asked if he could call in person as there was a matter he needed to discuss too delicate for the telephone.

'Is something wrong, Mr Alder?' Jean asked. She thought she heard a sigh.

'I would prefer to talk to you in person. Would it be possible this morning? Around eleven thirty? I have an hour's window, if that isn't inconvenient.'

Jean briefly wondered if Mr Alder was also calling on his mobile phone.

'I was considering going out . . .' she said, thinking aloud.

'The matter will not take long. It is rather important or I would never have intruded.'

'You've talked me into it. Would you like to stay for a bite of lunch?' Jean asked. 'Just a sandwich. I could easily rustle something up.'

'That will not be necessary,' Mr Alder responded in a slightly cooler voice. 'And I do feel I need to warn you that your aunt has no knowledge of this telephone call.'

'Well then, I shan't tell her. I shan't breathe a word to any living soul, Mr Alder. My lips are tightly sealed until you arrive.'

Smiling to herself but annoyed, as soon as Mr Alder had replaced his receiver Jean tapped out Freida's number.

'Hello, poo-face, are you polishing your dildo?' she said as soon as the receiver was picked up.

'I'm sorry,' came a cold voice, 'I think you've a wrong number.'

'Oh, I do apologize, I wanted to speak to Freida.'

The receiver was thumped down. In the background Jean heard voices that did not sound exactly happy.

'Darling! I haven't heard from you in yonks! Are you in town for long? Come over straight this minute so I can ravish you on the kitchen floor. I haven't had a good bonk in months.'

There was another background sound of a door slamming shut.

'Sorry, Jean,' Freida briskly added. 'That was Mandy. She's been threatening to move in. A ghastly, depressing thought. She's already criticized the wallpaper in the guest bedroom and suggested we get a new carpet for the hall. Damn all dykes. How are you? What's wrong? You only call me poo-face when you're upset.'

Jean explained about Mr Alder's call.

'Do you want me to come over?'

'No, I don't see you need to.'

'Please, please. It would give me the best excuse.'

'Well, look. Come over later. I'm expecting Mr Alder around eleven thirty. Come around one. I'll make lunch. It's probably nothing, but he was rather offy on the phone.'

'Definitely the anal retentive type. I suspected as much when I met the dear man.'

Jean began to laugh. The one time Freida had met Mr Alder she had persistently squeezed his upper arm in a suggestive manner until he had begun to perspire. She had kept asking him if he loved his mother and whether he thought incest should be made more socially acceptable. Freida had taken an instant dislike to him.

'I shall go out directly and spend as much as I possibly can in Kensington High Street before I arrive,' she said. 'Extravagance, dear Lady Jean, is what one needs after last night. It was tears before bedtime the entire evening. Mandy will have to down tools and depart. See you soon.'

Jean sat out in the garden in one of the wicker chairs, close to Henry the Fifth's grave. Christopher had done an excellent job of burial. On top of the small mound he had planted a miniature bush that had tiny white flowers. The other Henry graves were spread out along the perimeter of the walls. Some of them were now completely hidden from sight in the undergrowth. Mrs Meiklejohn had ventured out into her own garden. Jean could see only the top of her head as she slowly made her way down the central path. Mrs Meiklejohn was of short stature with a face like thunder and suffered from stiff joints. She favoured long pleated skirts, had been born in Stepney and failed to disguise her working-class accent.

'Good morning,' Jean called cheerfully. 'A lovely Spring day!'

Mrs Meiklejohn did not reply, or at least Jean did not hear a response. The woman was exceedingly dour. Her husband had been from South Africa. He had divorced her ten years ago and returned home. There'd been no children. Freida referred to Mrs Meiklejohn as the Lady Maggot.

Jean was languishing in the bath upstairs when she heard Freida arrive at one thirty. Freida had her own set of keys and still called out, as she entered, 'Cooee, it's the Devil's Dyke,' which was nothing short of tasteless.

She had first used the expression back when Jean's elderly parents were living once again at Acacia Road. They had, for many years, lived near Devil's Dyke outside Brighton until they were unable to manage.

Freida was sitting in the morning-room when Jean came downstairs. Surrounding her on the floor sat numerous cardboard shopping bags, each one sporting the name of an expensive designer shop.

'Well, I see *you've* had a good time,' Jean said in a clipped tone, leaning to kiss Freida on the cheek. 'I've made sandwiches. Have you eaten?'

'I am famished. I am poorer by such a disgusting amount I shall need therapy to adjust and at least two swift gins. Did the hotel homo show?'

'I wish you wouldn't use that word. It's insulting.'

'What, hotel? You are tetchy, sister. You're annoyed at me, aren't you? I know. I promise to stop yelling out when I let myself in. There, satisfied? Come, sit down, I'll waive the gins while you tell all.'

Jean sat down heavily. For a moment she passed her hands over her face, drawing them down and peering across at Freida over the tops of her fingers.

'The hotel wants Aunt Dizzy out,' she said bluntly.

'Oh dear, oh, oh dear. I had a feeling it might be that. Has she been a naughty old girl *again?*'

Jean drew her hands down into her lap where they sat writhing. She smiled at Freida's expression of feigned concern.

'Oh, it's several things really. Aunt Dizzy's age. They certainly aren't happy with her any longer. And the hotel's going to be closed for complete refurbishment. Three months. So Aunt Dizzy will have to move out in the interim. But in the long term, as Mr Alder so carefully explained, it would not be conducive to sound public relations if Auntie were to stay on.'

Freida pulled a face and hissed through her perfect teeth.

'She's spent a fortune staying there, all this time. That rotten little toad.'

'Oh, it's not his fault. He's only under orders. They've recommended a home, in Kent. Mr Alder gave me a brochure.' Jean went to offer it to Freida, picking it up from the coffee-table.

Freida merely stared at it and shuddered. 'You can't, Jean. You mustn't even consider it. Not for Doo Lally. She'd pine away within a month. You know how she feels.'

'It sounds terribly grand. *En suite* everything, resident doctors on twenty-four-hour call, indoor swimming-pool. Just like a hotel, really. Lovely gardens.'

'It would still be a home, for goodness' sake,' Freida almost snapped. 'Really, she could come to live with me if you feel you can't have her here. You know I adore the old parrot. She's a rare treasure.'

Jean stood up and moved towards the door leading into the kitchen. She was grinning.

'I've just decided,' she said softly. 'Aunt Dizzy shall come here. I'll work it all out. I should have had her living here years ago.' Jean left the room and made her way into the kitchen.

As she was removing plastic wrap from the plates of sandwiches, Freida called, 'You know, sweetness, she told me once that the only enjoyable sex she ever engaged in was with other women. She seduced a parlour maid one afternoon while the gentlemen of the house were playing cricket only a few feet away.'

Jean did not reply. She was quietly downing a tumbler of gin.

THREE

When Jean is away from the house and the Fallen Nun is also absent, the rooms and the hallways appear to grow darker and even more shadowed than usual. The house sits waiting for its mistress to return, like a devoted dog. Alert and listening and a little stressed, the walls seem to diminish, to shrink inwards as if seeking something that is missing. There is a kind of sadness in the morning-room and in the kitchen, and the air elsewhere is thick with what might well be melancholy. Dust hovers like a presence. There is the occasional sound of foundations settling or a soft crackling as if the unused electricity in the walls is chattering to itself. Christopher has noticed this. He has not said anything for fear of being thought even more queer than he already thinks he is.

In the past the house was filled with laughter, though not all the time. There was silence too, but the silence was fleeting. There were tantrums from children, juvenile screaming, adult chatter and much music. Family garden parties were held on the lawn during summer days. Along with casual games of croquet and badminton and no-rules cricket, Jean might be seen, a child – or two – beside her, dressed in pastel summer finery, on her knees weeding or planting or simply admiring the beds of flowers that are now gone and have never been replaced. The family would gather on the lawn every Sunday during the summer or in the Green Room when the weather changed. Charades would be ritually played after sumptuous lunches of beef and Yorkshire pudding and perfectly roasted potatoes with Brussels sprouts. Opened wine and fruit juice bottles sat empty on every surface. There were birthday parties, the occasional wake. Impressive guests came who had appeared on television or were in the theatre. There was love. There was momentary hate and triumph; there were mood swings and arguments and hope.

Now, the house is, more often than not, a forlorn though dignified place, like a seaside boarding-house in perpetual winter. Where once lived, long before the first Barries appeared, an architect with an artificial leg, a failed Irish female poet, two elderly gentlemen who created local scandal by regularly walking along the high street hand in hand, there now exists an air of desolation. There were families, in the mid eighteenth century, with servants and daily helps and sexual frigidity. An elderly woman during the Second World War lived not unhappily in the garden shed for a time after her own house near by was bombed. The garden shed is long gone. Children born in the house on Acacia Road are gone, have lived their lives elsewhere and died. The house has seen so many within its walls. In a sense, they are still there. Christopher Harcourt is convinced of this. The house is not peaceful in its present age, for it has never before been so quiescent. On days and nights when rain falls, it is not only the Fallen Nun's rooms on the uppermost floor that seep with damp. Downstairs, excessive condensation trickles slowly down the windows and the walls, as if the house is weeping.

It was early Friday morning. Jean, having had a bath, the first of several she indulged in every day, was examining the boxes of records in the front reception room. It would be a suitable place in which to set up a small bedsitting-room for Aunt Dizzy. It was a large plain room with tall windows and a high corniced ceiling. There was an ornate, aged vanity unit in one corner. Being at the front of the house, the room would be quiet. Jean smiled thinly at the thought. The entire house was quiet.

She was brooding over Freida's use of 'Devil's Dyke'. It was typical of Freida to keep on using the place-name as an expression, which amused her cynical mind, when Jean's parents were dead. It was a reminder, something other people created which induced hurt. Freida had promised to refrain from using the expression several times. The memory it brought Jean caused pain after dark. Nights like the one just gone. There were three empty bottles of Tanqueray in the kitchen, sitting in a row on the floor as if waiting to be part of a game of skittles. Christopher would see to them. He would say nothing. He had stared at her rather oddly when he'd arrived earlier. His eyes were slightly puffed as if he had been crying. She did not make any comment about them. He was out in the garden cutting the grass, using the old hand mower that had belonged to Jean's grandfather. Jean refused to buy a petrol-driven mower, as Christopher had once suggested. Its sound would antagonize.

Jean had sipped gin and wandered the rooms of the house for most of the night, trying to avoid her personal ghosts. The gin made her weep at first, and recollection was edged and focused like newly sharpened knives until the alcohol, trickling through her system, took control. Memory faded then, until there was nothing to be afraid of. Some nights she would gaily sing or loudly play her own music and laugh at it or play others' music and be overcome with envy. She listened to Nina Simone quite often. For years, in her youth, she believed she was in love with Nina Simone. Jean's solo drinking parties had become a pattern, and they became something to look forward to because into the drunken state euphoria would eventually appear. She did not grow maudlin or depressed, as people who drank alone are generally said to become. Jean would dance as well as sing.

She would laugh and cry out before falling asleep, and in the morning, when she awoke, the house would seem perfectly at ease with her. A perfect place to be in, just as it had been, before.

Just after ten thirty the doorbell rang. Jean had moved the boxes of records in the reception room, lining them up against one wall. She had vacuumed the floor. The boxes were ready to be moved out and sent off into storage.

Aunt Dizzy stood on the steps, purple straw hat askew and face flushed. She had brought two suitcases with her and a gigantic bunch of iris blooms and a bottle of gin, the latter items threatening to fall from her precarious grasp.

'I was about to leave to come and collect you, Auntie!' Jean exclaimed.

'Am I late? Is Freida here yet? The taxi driver was drunk. I can't go on coming here in taxis, Jean. One of the drivers will kidnap me one day and then where will we be? It's all too much for an old white lady.'

Aunt Dizzy's lips were turned down at the corners. There were beads of perspiration amongst the carefully bleached hairs of her upper lip. She appeared close to tears. As cheerfully as she could, Jean relieved her of the flowers and the unwrapped gin, ushering her inside. On the street the taxi driver began to press his horn. Realizing that Aunt Dizzy wouldn't have offered the man a tip, Jean attended to that before carrying the suitcases into the hall. The driver did indeed appear to be drunk. He had smiled and bared his teeth at her in an obscene kissing gesture as she walked towards the cab. In thin-lipped fury she threw a pound coin through the opened side window and glared at the man until he drove off.

Aunt Dizzy had collapsed into an armchair in the morning-room. She was powdering her face. Now back in control and looking none the worse for anything, she said cheerfully, 'There's a young man in your garden, Jean. He's particularly ugly. I think he's up to no good. He hasn't seen me.'

'It's Christopher. You remember. Christopher Harcourt. He comes to help out on Fridays. You and he like each other.'

'*Do* we?'

Aunt Dizzy had spilt face powder down the front of her suit jacket. When not dressed in fake Victorian splendour, she sometimes favoured matching pleated skirts and jackets and long necklaces of real pearls. She had had her wig cut short and blue-rinsed. It looked stiff with hairspray. Aunt Dizzy was totally bald.

'You should never wear trousers, Jean,' she said, looking up. 'Your bottom doesn't suit them now you're well into your fifties.'

'Cup of tea, Auntie?'

'Vodka would be valium, but tea will cover the tideline,' Aunt Dizzy recited. It was one of numerous stock phrases that she repeated over and over again. Jean knew all of them off by heart. As she turned to leave the room Aunt Dizzy was peering out the french windows.

'*Who* did you say that lad is?' she asked.

'Christopher. Christopher Harcourt.'

'He's revoltingly tall, isn't he? *How* old did you say he was?'

'He's seventeen, Auntie,' Jean called back over her shoulder as she entered the kitchen, about to put the iris blooms into water. 'You'll remember him in a moment. You just rest.'

'Well, he's bloody ugly,' Jean heard her mutter. Aunt Dizzy had taken up swearing after reading an article in a magazine that convinced her it would help with stress and memory loss. She had fallen asleep when Jean returned with tea and biscuits on a tray. Her head resting against the right wing of the armchair, while Jean had been out of the room she had reapplied bright lipstick. Her mouth was opening and closing as she gently snored. The carmine of her lips contrasted oddly with her yellowed teeth. She had recently had new dentures tinted to look as if they were all her own in case, she had explained at the time, someone tried to steal them from her hotel room during the night. Most of the staff were foreign.

Christopher was preparing a light lunch in the kitchen when the telephone rang. Jean had eventually helped Aunt Dizzy upstairs to one of the guest rooms, where she was now snoring happily beneath an eiderdown quilt, stockings removed, teeth and wig removed and face shining from a moisturizing soap wash. She had acted utterly exhausted, as if she had not slept the night before. Jean was about to find out that this was true.

'Mr Alder!' Jean responded cheerfully when she answered the call and heard his voice, just as if she was genuinely pleased to hear from him.

'Has your aunt arrived safely, Miss Barrie?'

'Why, yes, she has, but she's fast asleep. I'm afraid I wouldn't like to disturb her. Is there anything I can do for you, Mr Alder? May I pass on a message?'

In the ensuing brief silence Jean could hear background voices, whispering.

'We were wondering,' Mr Alder went on almost breathlessly but coldly into the receiver, 'when someone would be along to collect everything else.' There was a distinct note of sarcasm in his voice.

'I don't know what you mean. Have I missed something?'

There was more whispering then a clunking sound which lasted several seconds.

'I'm terribly sorry,' Mr Alder said. 'I was led to believe that everything had been prearranged. Your aunt appears to have moved out of her own accord. My foyer is, shall we say, *over-burdened* with numerous suitcases and boxes. I assumed that a carrier would have been along by now, to collect.'

'You never cease to surprise me, Mr Alder. I know nothing about Auntie . . . about my aunt, Miss Barrie, moving out *today*. It's all rather sudden, isn't it? I thought we had agreed to –'

'Your aunt apparently decided herself to leave this morning. Or, rather, yesterday evening. She spent the entire night – or indeed most of it – inveigling my staff into packing and bringing down everything she owns, which now sits about cluttering up the entrance to my hotel. Unfortunately I was not here at all last night and I have only just returned. Would you please arrange immediate collection or I shall be forced to take steps.'

'Steps, Mr Alder?' Jean asked in a cold, steady voice. 'Is that to be taken as a threat?'

Christopher had wandered out into the hall. He was standing staring at her. It was a second or two before she realized that the snuffling sound was his crying. Tears poured down his face in a salty torrent. He was clutching the breadknife in one hand. His lips looked even larger and wider than ever. His eyes were bloodshot and now badly swollen.

'I am not threatening you, Miss Barrie,' Mr Alder went on. 'I do apologize. You obviously knew nothing of this latest development. I am an honourable man. I am sorry if I caused alarm. I shall immediately arrange delivery of your aunt's possessions, for this afternoon. It will not be a problem. She has paid her bill, I am just informed, in full and said her goodbyes. To all, except to me.'

Christopher had let the breadknife drop to the floor. He drew his hands up to cover his face. His shoulders heaved in what appeared to be absolute grief. Through the fashionable, horizontal rips in the knees of his jeans was revealed such white flesh that Jean found herself staring at it as she tried to listen to Mr Alder's stutterings and apologies. He kept pausing and then repeating himself, just as he had done during his brief visit. Someone in the background was speaking urgently as if explaining things to him. His voice changed from coldness to agitation.

'. . . and I was not in full possession of the facts, I fear. I shall write to you immediately with a full explanation and an apology,' he was saying, when Jean's concentration diverted itself back to the telephone. Christopher had turned away and re-entered the kitchen, where she could hear him weeping uncontrollably.

'There's no need to write and apologize, nor explain, Mr Alder, but thank you,' Jean managed to say. 'I know my aunt can be difficult. Are you sure you can manage to have all her things sent today? There's no urgency at this end.'

'No trouble at all. I do need clearance, you understand. And may I add that indeed it was a pleasure to have had your aunt stay with us here these past few years. She has been particularly generous to my staff.'

There was more muffled whispering.

'And Miss Greco wishes to pass on her gratitude to your aunt for all her English lessons.'

The man appeared to be wanting to waffle on for ever. Jean managed to gush her own false gratitude and, interrupting him as he started off again, said goodbye.

Jean quickly replaced the receiver. She hurried down the hall and into the kitchen. The room was empty. The door leading out into the garden was open.

She found Christopher kneeling at Henry the Third's grave, which he had been clearing of weeds a foot high and undergrowth of several years. He was still weeping. Tendrils of mucus dangled from his weak chin. When he realized she was beside him he turned away and wiped a pale hand across his face. Jean fumbled in her trouser pocket and handed him a handkerchief.

'*Whatever* is the matter?' she asked, once he had loudly blown his nose and wiped his chin. Christopher glanced up and immediately began to cry again, his mouth opening so wide that Jean formed the incongruous thought that if two large cooking apples were to be inserted into it Christopher would be none the wiser. He was solely concentrated on his grief.

'It's nothing,' he managed to gasp. Then he grew perfectly still, staring down at Henry the Third's grave. Carefully he reached out to smooth the earth there with his long, thin and quite delicate fingers.

'I'd like to help,' Jean offered. 'Has someone died? Is your mother ill?'

After a moment Christopher gave a slight shudder, sniffed loudly and said in a small voice, 'It's my uncle. Uncle Fergus.'

'Oh dear. Has *he* died? Is he ill?'

Jean suddenly felt an overwhelming urge to laugh. She bit her tongue, mentally slapping her wrist. Freida, she thought. Freida would have laughed. Jean could not for the life of her recall whether Christopher had ever mentioned an uncle. She was still rather fazed by Mr Alder's telephone call. Christopher was shaking his head. He began to look almost angry. He suddenly scrambled to his feet and moved off down the garden, standing with his back to her, shoulders hunched. His fists, at his sides, were clenched.

'Well, if I can help in any way, Christopher. If you need to talk to someone . . . I'll be in the kitchen.'

Jean turned away. When she was half-way up the garden she heard him say, 'She caught us', and turned back.

Christopher was facing her. His face looked calmer, but now his hands twisted together in front of him as if he was in the act of washing them under a tap. '*She caught us,*' he repeated, whispering the words but an urgency to communicate in the tone. He stepped towards her. For a moment Jean was terrified he was about to rush forward and throw his arms about her. His eyes were all size and desperation.

'My Uncle. Uncle Fergus. Mother . . .' He stopped and just stood there, head lowered. 'She's thrown me out. She put all my things into plastic bags and made me give her back my keys and everything's up at the tube station being looked after.'

'I'll make tea,' Jean said. As Christopher's face again began to crumple she stepped back down the garden and took one of his hands. He was trembling. 'It'll be all right, come on. Don't cry any more. Aunt Dizzy's here. She'll cheer you up. She'll have remembered who you are by the time she wakes up.'

Christopher held her hand so tightly as they made their way back up across the newly mown grass that Jean could have sworn she felt one of her bones crack. Mrs Meiklejohn was watching from her upstairs drawing-room window. Her face, as usual, was devoid of any expression except for a reptilian curiosity.

FOUR

The Fallen Nun was never domiciled in a convent nor has she ever been a Catholic. It is a disrespectful title, bestowed on her by Freida, who is denied gossip by Miss Truman's ability to avoid contact, something she has managed to do cleverly ever since she moved in, after William Fitzpatrick, now Jean's ex-husband, moved out and instigated divorce. It was Freida's idea for Jean to take in a lodger. Just as it had been for Jean to keep her unmarried name. The former had not worked out as Freida anticipated. The Fallen Nun keeps entirely to herself. She comes and goes with stealth as if, Freida was convinced for at least three months, she *has* been in a convent and is therefore accustomed to creeping about and being sequestered. Jean has, at least, discovered that Catherine Truman attends an acting school. She is hoping to become a jobbing actress, a fact Jean keeps from Freida, who would undoubtedly claim that no one with the plain, homely features and lumpy figure of the Fallen Nun could possibly count on success. Freida is knowledgeable about and addicted to the theatre. She attends new plays at least once a fortnight and disagrees with every review she reads in the broadsheet press. The Fallen Nun, eventually accepted by Jean as a mildly inoffensive semi-recluse, is left to her own vices and virtues. She never receives visitors. She does not drink. She pays her rent and bills punctually. She is the very model of sobriety. Freida detests her.

•

There are signs that the house might be aware of change. The front hallway appears to be letting in more light during the day through the small glass panels of the door. The air seems less dusty. After dark, with more lights burning and more movement from new occupants, there is a slight glow. It is so minimal that even Christopher has not noticed. Voices do not echo. The foundations and wooden floors creak with a softer sound, and a touch of warmth does seem to emanate from the aged walls.

Christopher and Aunt Dizzy were playing Scrabble in the morning-room. The Scrabble board rested on a small rosewood table between them. The table had been made in 1826 by a craftsman whose descendants are buried in the local cemetery. Jean had no idea the table was a valuable antique.

'Hystricomorph *is* a word,' Aunt Dizzy was insisting. 'Porcupines are hystricomorphs. Look it up if you don't believe me. I'm not trying to trick you, Christopher. You young people are astonishingly ignorant.'

Christopher was listening for the doorbell. Despite the late hour he was hoping Uncle Fergus might call. He was not paying a great deal of attention. Jean was sleeping up in her room covered by a quilt that had been handmade by her great-grandmother. It was ten o'clock on a Thursday evening, six days after Aunt Dizzy and Christopher had moved in. Both of them were sleeping in guest rooms on the first floor. They shared a bathroom that separated their bedrooms. Aunt Dizzy had twice forgotten to lock the connecting door while she was taking a bath. Christopher had walked into the bathroom on the second night and seen Aunt Dizzy lying prone in a bathful of steaming hot water. He thought she was dead. Minus her wig and teeth and stark naked, it was not altogether surprising that he ran downstairs in a state of shock, only to find Jean in the arms of Anthony Hibbert, in the throes of struggling with his slightly drunken advances. Christopher had charged into the room and Jean had cried out and Christopher had shrieked in a particularly high voice and upstairs Aunt Dizzy had woken up. As she said later, she'd almost drowned from the noise below. It had given her such a fright she'd slid about in the bath like a small whale, causing much of the water to slop out on to the floor. The three of them, after Anthony Hibbert had left, apologizing profusely and red-faced, sat in the kitchen until two in the morning, playing Scrabble to calm their nerves. Ever since then Aunt Dizzy and Christopher were unable to resist playing Scrabble whenever a free hour presented itself. They gleefully shared their addiction like unsupervised children. Aunt Dizzy *had* eventually recalled who Christopher was and seemed rather pleased that he had also moved in.

'It's almost like the old days, Jean,' she kept saying. 'Before the bad time. I like a bit of life around this house. There wasn't much of it at the hotel.'

Jean had asked Christopher to move in the same afternoon that Aunt Dizzy's mountain of possessions had arrived, and Jean found out that Christopher had been made homeless by his own parents. Not believing him at first, she telephoned his mother, only to be told in a frigid and icy tone that Mrs Harcourt did not have a son any longer. Christopher had gone away and she never expected to see him again. Jean was stunned.

'Well, he is here with *me*, Mrs Harcourt,' she said, trying to control her astonishment and an urge to be rude. The woman had spoken with the finality of death. 'He has one of my guest rooms. If you happen to feel the need to speak to your son, do please call. He is dreadfully upset.'

Before she finished speaking Mrs Harcourt replaced her receiver.

Jean and Christopher had sat in the kitchen after she'd brought him in from the garden six days ago, bereft and crying. It took a full hour before he was able to tell her clearly what had happened, what had been going on. In the middle of his confession Aunt Dizzy had wandered in, having woken up and descended the stairs. Wearing little more than a vague smile and underwear, she prepared to make herself a pot of tea. It took her a little while to realize that she was not alone, but then she simply smiled delicately, placing the filled teapot and a mug on a tray when she was ready and departed the room gracefully, as if it was completely ordinary for an 81-year-old lady to walk about almost naked. Christopher, as he and Jean sat listening to Aunt Dizzy negotiate the stairs, began to snigger. Then he had a fit of hiccups and started to cry all over again.

'Uncle Fergus really *loves* me,' he explained after he'd calmed down and Jean had let go of his hands, which caused him to hold his fingers up and sniff at them. 'We've always got on well, even when I was small. I used to sit on his lap at family get-togethers. There's nothing wrong in what we do. Mother hates me. She'll never allow me back. Father won't, either. He always does what he's told.'

Mrs Harcourt had found Christopher lying fully clothed in the arms of her only brother which, as Jean pointed out, would have been a terrible shock for anyone, let alone Christopher's mother who was a devout Evangelical Christian.

'We were only kissing,' Christopher said in defence. 'We kiss a lot. We hold hands. I love Uncle Fergus. I've always loved him. I've wanted him to kiss me ever since I was fifteen.'

Jean had sympathized as best she could and simply let

Christopher talk. Words had eventually poured from his lips to rival the tears that had been flowing from his eyes. He had been secretly meeting Uncle Fergus for almost a year, he told her. He could not see that anything was wrong with that. They visited the cinema, the theatre, the Natural History Museum and the Wallace Collection, as well as having afternoon tea at Uncle Fergus's maisonette off Long Acre. 'It was destiny,' Christopher said. 'Uncle Fergus has always been alone and one of these days we'll be together, for ever.'

Jean was unable to know exactly what to say, except eventually to suggest that Christopher fetch his possessions from the tube station. She would make up one of the guest rooms for him.

'Only overnight,' she explained. 'I'm having to let Aunt Dizzy live here now. Your mother will come round. It's just been the shock, I expect.'

Now Christopher had been living at Acacia Road for almost a week. His father had telephoned and stiffly asked Jean if he could speak to his son.

'He said Mother's praying for me,' Christopher told Jean. 'She's got her whole church praying for me twice a day at special gatherings. Father wouldn't talk about Uncle Fergus. He clammed up and then put the phone down and cut me off.'

Since then Jean had found a cheque stuffed inside an envelope pushed through the letterbox. The cheque had been made out to cash and was attached to a note from Christopher's father who explained 'To Whom It May Concern' that the money was to cover Christopher's expenses. Jean had ripped up the cheque and said nothing to Christopher about it. The cheque had been for over two thousand pounds.

Christopher and Aunt Dizzy spent most of their time together, and Jean was able to leave them alone and not feel forced to keep an eye on either. Christopher, without being asked, slipped into the role of Aunt Dizzy's minder. He followed her about the house with a studied, serious devotion, making certain she was dressed properly in the mornings, preparing meals, cleaning up after her. In between, they played Scrabble. He had taken some days off studying.

Anthony Hibbert had telephoned to apologize for his sexual advances.

'I've no real excuse,' he admitted. 'Except that I fancy you. I was tired and pissed.'

'I'm old enough to be your mother,' Jean responded.

'So? Will you forgive me?'

'Nothing to forgive. Besides, I'm the one who should feel apologetic. To be perfectly honest, Anthony, I had rather lost interest in a memoir several months ago. I've been enjoying your company.'

Anthony Hibbert remained silent for only a few seconds.

'Oh, I've known about that for some time. About the memoir, I mean. So have the publishers. They gave up around a month ago. I've just enjoyed being with you too. Hope you don't mind.'

He promised to telephone after a forthcoming trip to Brussels. Jean had agreed to let him escort her one night to an opera or a ballet at Covent Garden. She knew so little about him. Naturally she was flattered. Anthony Hibbert was twenty-five years old with the confidence of someone ten years older.

When Jean came downstairs after her long early evening nap it was gone eleven o'clock. Christopher and Aunt Dizzy were quietly arguing in the morning-room, still playing Scrabble.

'If you place those bloody letters there you won't get such a high score,' she was saying as Jean entered the room. 'Do try something else, for heaven's sake. Moron.'

They did not even look up as Jean passed them, heading for the kitchen. She warmed milk and spooned cocoa into three mugs. She did not hear the faint sigh that appeared to come from the walls. In the morning-room Christopher glanced up towards the kitchen door and grinned. Jean waited for the milk to warm and considered telephoning Freida.

She had spent the morning telephoning plumbers and electricians and a decorator, then ordered an expensive orthopaedic bed for Aunt Dizzy's front room. The boxes of records had already gone, collected and now stored away in the north London warehouse where she sent everything there wasn't room for. Most of the furniture from the house William had owned before he'd married her was there along with much of what Aunt Dizzy had not wished to keep when she'd sold her own house. She had wanted a new bed, she'd told Jean, one with modern technology to help aged bones to rest and a restless mind to dream. The workmen were arriving in the morning to start renovating the front room. There was not a great deal to be done. Most of the furnishings were being delivered from the warehouse, items that Aunt Dizzy did want. Curtains, two Queen Anne chairs, an antique card-table for her and Christopher to play Scrabble on. A dressing-table with chair. She had given Jean a list. Jean had said little about why Christopher had moved in. There seemed little point in explaining. Jean had casually said that it was temporary, owing to Christopher's mother needing a break.

'Well, I am pleased,' Aunt Dizzy had responded. 'He's a lovely boy even if he is damned ugly. He speaks well of you, Jean.' She had invited one or two of the hotel staff to visit the house, once her new room was put in order, then cancelled the invitation. Jean had considered turning the other reception room into a bathroom, but Aunt Dizzy rather liked the idea of a stair-lift so she could use the upstairs bathroom.

'Much more fun than merely stepping across the hall,' she'd commented. 'Besides, I can pay visits to Miss Truman. The way you ignore her appalls me, Jean. It's not right.'

The telephone rang as the three of them were sipping cocoa.

'I'm terribly embarrassed to telephone so late,' came a high-pitched but melodic voice when Jean answered. 'But I've been led to believe that Mr Christopher Harcourt is there.'

'You must be Uncle Fergus,' Jean found herself saying.

'I am! How very flattering of you to recognize my voice!'

Jean was about to explain that she hadn't when Christopher appeared in the hall, staring intently at her. His face, normally pale, had gone a sickly shade. Jean held out the receiver and at his sudden look of terror she smiled and squeezed his arm.

'It's all right,' she whispered. 'It's your uncle. Talk for as long as you want.'

Christopher waited until she had gone back into the morning-room before he spoke. Jean closed the hall door. Aunt Dizzy had fallen asleep in her chair. She still clutched her cocoa and a lit cigar. Jean relieved her of both, gently waking her, then helped her up the stairs after locking the kitchen door and turning off all the lights except one. When she returned downstairs, having put Aunt Dizzy to bed and been lectured on the rudiments of denture hygiene and the best and worst cleaners of false teeth on the market, Christopher was still on the telephone. She could hear the murmer of his voice as she put her ear to the door panel. It was gone midnight when he sheepishly returned to the morning-room. He was agitated and wouldn't sit down.

'I don't suppose . . .' he said. He stopped and wrung his hands together in a gesture Jean had already observed numerous times, a nervous reaction that made him look older and of which he did not seem to be aware. He was also finding it difficult to look at her.

'Sit down,' she said slowly. 'Don't get yourself worked up. Now tell me what you want so we can all get to bed. It's late. Busy day tomorrow.'

Christopher sat opposite her. He stopped wringing his hands and stared across at her with his large brown eyes that did little to compensate for his weak chin and general appearance of the great unwashed.

'Uncle wants to know if he'll be allowed to visit me. Here. He's been keeping clear.'

'Of course he can. I've no problem with that, Christopher, no problem at all. I'd like to meet him. He could come for afternoon tea or a meal if he wants. Anything you decide.'

The relief on Christopher's face was astonishing. He sat back in the chair and put the palms of his hands together as if he was about to break into applause. He blinked rapidly.

'I want you to like him,' he whispered, dipping his head.

'I'm sure I shall. You are welcome to stay here, Christopher, for as long as you wish. I've just decided. No rules. You can come and go as you please. I'll get some keys cut. You've been a real boon to Aunt Dizzy. I am grateful. But don't let her take you over, that's all you need to promise. Now, it's terribly late and I'm terribly tired. I hope you're going back to college?'

Christopher nodded.

'Tomorrow,' he said. He stared at her, then suddenly stood up. Stepping across the room he knelt down at Jean's feet and, reaching for her hand, drew it to his lips.

Jean froze. She was not at all certain she liked the sensation of Christopher's lips on her skin. They felt rubbery. Cold, almost artificial. She sat rigidly. He remained kneeling there for a moment after letting go her hand. His eyes were closed. One solitary tear was coursing down his left cheek.

'This house loves you,' he whispered.

Then in a rushed movement he scrambled to his feet and turned, heading to the stairs and ascending them so silently and swiftly it left her a little breathless. There was not a sound after that. Jean continued to sit in her chair without moving. She thought about Freida. She thought about William, now apparently back living in London. She thought about her daughter and her son and her parents. She remained sitting in the chair for a long time, in near darkness, one hand in her lap caressing the other in a gentle rhythm.

FIVE

We were an average family, all things considered, Jean had nervously and reluctantly said into Anthony Hibbert's minicorder, which she had knocked on to the floor by accident as soon as they had settled. Later, she was to cringe over saying it.

William had an established reputation as a financial adviser, with a business in the City. We had the house. There was Grandfather's cottage in Wales, though we rarely went down there. We were comfortable, not too complacent, unaware of anything much outside the family. Jared and Gemma attended good schools. Socially we were busy. Hurrying through our lives, cushioned by the Barrie wealth. At this point Jean stops speaking and begins to laugh.

The tape is stopped and then restarted.

William once said that he had married my entire family. My parents lived in Brighton when the children were small. They'd gone down there with the idea to semi-retire and bought an old detatched house near Devil's Dyke. They came up to town every weekend, sometimes staying with Father's sister Elizabeth – Aunt Dizzy. They missed London. It was long before Auntie sold her own house and moved into the hotel. The entire clan – or rather mine – gathered at Acacia Road every weekend, summer and winter. At first, when my singing career looked as though it was about to take off, Mother showed her disapproval, which she'd hidden. Everyone had treated my singing as an affectionate joke. Mother was terribly severe about it, terrified that any success I might encounter would remove me from them. None of them could quite believe I would succeed. When my first album rocketed within days of its release, things did begin to change. I'd recorded two singles before that. They'd both flopped miserably, never sold. I've a boxful in the front room I rarely admit to being there. After the album came out the phone never seemed to stop ringing. My agent of the time called, every day. So did the record company. I did small concerts in out-of-the-way places, made appearances. So many interviews. Then the two awards. Up there, on the mantel, gathering dust. It was a sudden opening up of something I'd longed for, all my adult life, to be a blues singer but a good one. And it came about, amidst all the unstoppable family business that carried on as usual. There, that's the truncated version!

The house was rarely empty. William had a great number of friends who regularly came to dinner. He had relatives in Canada who used to fly over and stay. Now they stay away in droves. William's own parents were not that close. They also lived down in Brighton, or rather in Hove, but didn't get along well with Mother and Father. William came from a more conventionally strict background than mine. His sister had been an actress for some years. Dead now. The black sheep, she was. Excommunicated Elaine, Will called her. From a long line of Fitzpatricks going back to secular roots in Ireland. William's mother was horrified over my singing success. She'd never forgiven me for insisting I be known as Jean Barrie after Will and I married. She was terribly cold. I'd been singing at the odd venue for some years by the time I married Will. His parents came to the wedding but left straight afterwards.

Jared was precocious as a boy. My first born. He and Gemma were close as children, not so noticeably when they became teenagers. They had a nanny when they were small. Later came a *succession of au pairs: Swedish, Italian, one from Spain who stole money. I was never happy about the au pairs, but I was away such a lot by then, travelling, giving concerts everywhere I was asked. I forgave William when I discovered he'd been having an affair with one of the Swedish girls. Aunt Dizzy was the only one I confided in over that. No one else found out. She's probably entirely forgotten about it now, bless her. That was a difficult time.* She pauses.

The tape is switched off, then back on.

Aunt Dizzy was so vivacious and energetic when the children were small! Always at the house during the week. Organized everything, came over when I was away. Gemma adored her. Jared decided by the age of ten that he wanted to become a veterinarian. Lord knows where that came from. Gemma had no idea what she wanted to do. Her ideas changed like the wind. She went through plans to study law, to become a barrister, a film star and a doctor – oh, there were so many changes in her as she grew up. A strange child. Very bossy but sweetly so. For two years she professed to hating Jared. He was forever playing pranks on her. Putting acorns in her shoes, tying shoelaces together, convincing local boys from the estate up the road that Gemma fancied them, or whatever the expression was they used back then. Encouraging them to call at the house. She threw a knife at Jared once, one evening in the kitchen. Missed him by inches. The mark's still there, on the cupboard door.

William was rarely home during the week, even in the evenings. He had a small flat over near Westminster, where he sometimes stayed overnight. He was always home at the weekends – or mostly – when the family gathered. There were very few outsiders, you understand, in the early days. Everyone was what you might call family-fixated. We were rather inward-looking. Introspective, is that the word? And my career did make waves and created change, as I said. I was eventually to become known, popular, in demand, independent of the family. People stopped by more and more often. The house got to be like Euston Station. Fortunate that my success did not really begin to take over until the children were older and able to adapt. Gemma went off to boarding-school at one stage and stayed there exactly one term. She hated it, missed the house, the weekend parties, the excitement of Mother becoming a star! Jean laughs, then stops suddenly. *We threw so many dinner parties, it was like opening a restaurant. I began to drink.*

The tape stops.

'Is this what you *really* want?' Jean asked Anthony Hibbert one evening after he had listened to one of the tiny tapes, checking it. 'It's all so ordinary. I sound smug and I think I've contradicted myself somewhere, on one of the other tapes.'

'Just chat,' he told her. 'Tell little stories. Reminisce. I'll do the rest. I can check back with you for particular dates and facts.'

'I never kept a diary. I told you that.'

'It doesn't necessarily matter. Speak about anything that comes to mind. The two awards, if you want. How you were able to combine success with family life.'

'But that's just it. I didn't.'

'The extra notes you've promised to write will help.'

Jean sipped at her tumbler of gin and stared at him without saying anything else.

Jared sweetened, as he grew older, if that's the word I mean. Maybe not. He was never sour . . . he was self-assured, intelligent. Nothing namby-pamby about Jared. He and Gemma seemed to swop personalities. Whereas she'd been sweetness and light as a child and far too trusting, if rather fickle and temperamental, with Jared consistently up to no good with his pranks, as they grew older they took on each other's behaviour. Odd, really. I might be imagining that. It wasn't something I noticed at the time. Perhaps I wouldn't have said that now, if they were still . . .

The tape stops, then restarts.

Jared once found a blackbird's nest in the garden, with three tiny corpses inside it. He secretly wrapped it up in pink tissue paper, placed it in a cardboard box and decorated the box with glitter and paper cut-outs of hearts. He kept it hidden until Gemma's birthday. She had a party that year, in the garden – just out there – and when it came time for her presents he made a grand entrance and handed his gift to her, all smiles and grand gestures. Her little friends were all agog, giggling and whispering as Gemma opened the gift. Dreadful, it was dreadful. Gemma had hysterics. Screamed the place down, made everyone go home. She would not speak to Jared for two months. Hated him. Hated him!

They both equally adored my parents, would do anything to get us to all go down to Brighton. Jared even phoned a minicab service once, in a disguised voice, ordering a taxi to take four 'adults', as he explained, down there on a visit as a surprise. He and Gemma got dressed and ready as if Will and I had arranged the entire thing. Terrible boy. The pranks – that kind of behaviour – carried on right throughout his early teens as well. He was relentless if Gemma showed any signs of interest in boys. The pranks would escalate. A terrible thing to admit, but I sometimes did wonder if he loved Gemma in a little too unbrotherly way. Is that a word, unbrotherly? He had a fixation on chalk when he was about seven or eight. Stole pieces from school and kept them in a shoe box under his bed. One Saturday night, terribly late, he crept out of the house and into the street and wrote in huge let-

*ters along the tarmac: GEMMA FITZPATRICK IS IN LOVE
WITH ARCHIBALD DOOLAN AND WANTS HIM TO MARRY
HER. Poor little Archibald was an excruciatingly shy, unfortunate boy who stuttered and came from a broken home. Bright red
hair, face covered in freckles. I was so angry over that with Jared.
It must have taken him an age to write the words along the road,
a foot high. It's little wonder he wasn't run over. And on Sunday
mornings families would gather along the pavement to chat,
catch up on news, something that certainly wouldn't happen
nowadays. Jared took Gemma out there once the stage was set
and neighbours had had time to read the message. So cruel,
really, but Jared thought it a huge, huge prank. Gemma was in
floods of tears over that one. She did forgive Jared, eventually.
And she wrote a sweet little note to Archibald Doolan, insisting
he came round for tea. She sat in here with him, on that chair
next to yours, and served flavoured milk and sticky buns, telling
him sincerely that her brother was insane and about to be taken
off and locked away. The tragedy of it was that Archibald Doolan
believed her and went home in floods of tears. I had to phone his
mother.*

'This is excellent,' Anthony Hibbert told Jean. 'It's those little
stories that we can use to illustrate what was to come.'

'Have you done this often?' Jean asked him brusquely, deliberately changing the subject. 'You can't have. You're very young.
I am impressed. You've got me talking about things I thought I'd
forgotten. I'm not sure I even remember things as they really
were.'

'It's to help you bring it all together,' he said. 'I'm sorry if that
sounds rather arrogant. Manipulative? And yes, I have done this
before. My age isn't relevant.'

'Oh dear, I'm sorry. I didn't mean . . . You do seem young. Or is it that I'm so much older. Everyone seems younger these days. Oh Lord. You've flustered me now. To be honest, I'm not really enjoying this at all. I know it's important . . .'

Neither Gemma nor Jared were all that impressed with my singing career. Not really. They were both too preoccupied with their friends and problems. I did as much as I could to keep it separate from what went on at home. I was away such an awful lot, for weeks sometimes. I guess that's when the drinking started to get worse. William noticed, Aunt Dizzy noticed. Will began to give me little lectures. I suppose it was the pursuit of true success that started the disintegration between Will and I, however hackneyed that sounds. And hindsight is a disturbing thing. My singing and being away did pull Will and I apart. It began to seem as if I had two separate lives. I made friends outside the family, I took on another persona. I was not Mother, or Mummy, not William's wife, out there. I was Jean Barrie. Blues singer. Lady Jean, eventually. A fan once referred to William, as she was talking at me, as Mr Barrie.

The entire family got involved and enthused when we heard I was to be given the two awards. Well, one. The other was a complete surprise. Most Promising Female Vocalist and then Best Female Vocalist, the same night. It caused some controversy. We went to the awards dinner together, along with Aunt Dizzy and two spinster aunts of Will's who were over from Canada. Oh, of course and Freida, too. It was an extraordinary evening. The children were hardly children by that time, but they were in awe of the whole thing. It's something I can't talk about without crying. I'm sorry. Can we . . . ?

The tape stops, then restarts.

Sales rocketed. I was invited on to a couple of chat shows on the BBC. There were plans for a documentary in which I was to take part. For several years after that I did forget who I was to the children, to William. I became a stranger to them. What if it had all happened when the children were small? Babies? Yet the thought never occurred to me. Not then, not when it was happening. It was exciting. Invigorating. For a time I left those I loved most behind me. I became a celebrity. Jean stops speaking, laughs, then is silent. The tape keeps running. *More and more often I wasn't here at the weekend gatherings. I'd be in New York or Manchester or recording some new damn album. The 'social' drinking went on. If only I'd known . . . I'm sorry. We'll have to stop.*

The tape ends.

'How would you like to approach what happened down in Wales?' Anthony Hibbert gently asked her one night. They were sitting upstairs in the Green Room – the drawing-room. It was late, almost eleven thirty on a Tuesday. They'd enjoyed a salad that Christopher had made and steak that Jean had grilled. Jean stared down at her hands and didn't reply to Anthony Hibbert's question. The telephone downstairs had stayed quiet all evening. No Freida. No Aunt Dizzy worrying about something like her teeth or her 'medicinal' stockings. The house remained hushed, as if it were listening. The Fallen Nun was away, holidaying in the Algarve. Several brief interviews had already been recorded by then, Jean dismissing most as being a waste of time and effort. She had talked with less and less enthusiasm into the minicorder while Anthony Hibbert sat opposite, not always looking at her and sometimes browsing through the few pages of notes she had given him. Her anxiety and discomfort had begun to escalate each time he placed the minicorder in front of her. She did not reveal how she felt. She knew the taped interviews were false and forced. Her words sounded unnatural.

She hadn't lied. She could not find the courage to ask him to stop.

After her long silence he did not ask the question again. A half-hour went by of mostly silence and then he was leaving. In the hall she said, 'I'm not going to talk about Wales at all. I've just decided. It's too painful, too difficult. I am sorry. You have access to newspaper reports. That's the best I can do – that's all I can do. What we've already done. You can try to change my mind, I suppose.'

He had gone to put his arms around her, to hug her, but she pulled back, avoiding his gaze. She watched him as he crossed the paving stones and went up the steps and out into the street. After he drove off she walked back indoors and switched off all the lights. Settling in the front room with a bottle of vodka, she drank herself, not for the first time, into oblivion.

SIX

Jean had tried to telephone Freida several times. There was never any reply. Her answerphone was not in use. In the post had arrived a brief note on headed notepaper, from William, asking Jean to call him. She hadn't. It was eight days since Aunt Dizzy and Christopher had moved in. They were out together, taking a walk in Regent's Park. Aunt Dizzy seemed filled with an energy Jean had not previously noticed. Always having talked a great deal, now she was also much more physically active. When Christopher was not meeting his Uncle Fergus or attending lectures, he and Aunt Dizzy were rarely apart, venturing out for short walks, visiting art galleries or the cinema. Uncle Fergus was coming for afternoon tea. Out of character, Jean had baked a chocolate cake, which Christopher had iced. There were cucumber and tomato sandwiches, two bowls of fresh asparagus with hollandaise sauce and three choices of tea. Christopher meticulously laid everything out in the drawing-room upstairs before leaving the house with Aunt Dizzy on his arm, explaining apologetically to Jean that Uncle Fergus was particular in everything, especially afternoon tea.

'He's really looking forward to meeting you,' Christopher said. 'I've told him all about Aunt Elizabeth, too, and her living here now.'

There had been no more telephone calls from Christopher's parents. Jean had sent a card suggesting they visit or that she go to see them to discuss Christopher's immediate future. There had been no response. Christopher had seen his father walking past the house twice on the pavement opposite. He had stopped to stare across at the windows before moving on, Christopher, with lips trembling, explained.

'He uses a walking-stick with a gold handle. Just in case you see anyone hanging about.'

Mr and Mrs Harcourt were elderly. They had married late after an engagement that lasted fifteen years. Christopher had grown up being told by his mother that his birth had been a regrettable accident.

Work had been completed on Aunt Dizzy's new front room. Deep pile carpet had been laid, the walls had been painted mushroom, new electrical sockets and plumbing had been seen to. The furniture, along with the new bed, was installed. Jean kept the windows open during the day, while the smell of paint faded. Aunt Dizzy did not approve of the room. Jean planned to move her in from upstairs as soon as she was able. Aunt Dizzy, however, had made it perfectly clear she wanted to remain upstairs and now refused to discuss the matter at all. She was fully determined to get her own way.

Jean was upstairs in her bedroom dressing, thinking about Catherine Truman, when the doorbell rang. The Fallen Nun had returned from the Algarve. She had left a letter on the hall table announcing that she was moving out. *I've been happy living here with you,* she wrote, *but I have found myself a room in Belsize Village, to be closer to my fiancé.* She went on to say, in a three-page explanation, that she was to be married soon to a man who loved her deeply, who was planning to take her to live in California, where she was to have a lead role next year in a major film opposite Kevin Bacon. All her hard work had paid off, she wrote. *I will try to see you before I leave, but I'm wretchedly*

busy. If I don't manage to, then I hope you will be happy always.
Inside the envelope was a large cheque to cover several weeks'
rent and bills. The amount was excessive.

Standing on the front steps when she answered the doorbell
stood a tall, thin, slack-jawed man with a moustache. Jean knew
instinctively that it was Uncle Fergus. He was wearing a canary-
yellow three-piece suit that looked 1930s in style if not in age
and immaculately pressed. There was a pink rosebud in the
lapel. Uncle Fergus wore a monocle in his left eye. Jean immediately thought: P. G. Wodehouse. In his arms he was carrying a
bunch of pink carnations wrapped in heavy chartreuse tissue
paper, which he thrust at her as if it were a weapon.

'Exquisite Jean Barrie!' he warbled. 'Lady Jean! At last we
meet! The flowers are for you, dear personage. I do trust I am
not late? I was overcome by horripilation in the taxi, so I
vacated it. I walked from the cricket grounds. Such a splendid
day, the air so crisp, so clean. The trees are burgeoning – as they
tend to do in spring.'

Jean had a fleeting urge to curtsy. She smiled hesitantly and
ushered Uncle Fergus into the hall.

'Christopher and Aunt Dizzy aren't back from their walk, so
you aren't late at all.'

'Oh, horrors. Then I must be early. Quite unforgivable. But
never mind, for I am here and what a distinct pleasure it is for us
all. Christopher has not stopped talking about your good self
nor of your aunt. I dare say he feels he has found a wee haven
here, away from that detestable sister of mine and her pin-
cushion of a husband.'

He kept on talking as he followed Jean down the hall and
into the morning-room. She'd taken the flowers and carried
them through into the kitchen.

'You know, I've often thought to buy a small property over this way. I have a modest, minuscule bivouac off Long Acre, but I long for a little garden like your own. Living where I do is all very well, but I undeniably miss such delight as a garden. A civilized thing, having one's own garden.'

Still talking as Jean came back into the morning-room, he was peering out through the french windows, hands thrust into the pockets of his jacket. His speech was comparable to recitation.

'My dear mother, bless her spirit in heaven, insisted that the family had a country retreat, to which I was trundled down every year of my childhood. As the older son I inherited it. I've been considering inviting you and your aunt down there, once summer spreads its splendour upon us. A glorious spot in Cheshire. I am greatly, greatly grateful that Christopher had you to turn to in his hour of darkness. In the circumstances need I say more?'

'Do sit down,' Jean said. 'I'm sure Christopher won't be long. They won't have walked far.'

After Uncle Fergus had edged his thin frame down into an armchair he continued to gaze out through the french windows and fell silent, ignoring her. Jean returned to the kitchen, after hovering. She pretended to be preparing the afternoon tea, rattling cups and noisily refilling the kettle after quietly emptying it. She was rather relieved when she heard Christopher and Aunt Dizzy entering the front door.

'Wolves should *never* be kept in such a small environment,' Aunt Dizzy was saying. 'It's cruel, Christopher, cruel. There's no two ways about it. Wolves need freedom. Freedom is not merely the reserve of us fortunate, fragile mortals.'

Jean stepped back into the morning-room, drying her hands on a towel. Uncle Fergus had got up from the chair and was nervously posed, his head turned to the hall door. His hands were again thrust into the pockets of his canary-yellow jacket. His monocle hung from a silver chain at his waist. There was an expression on his face of someone who was being hunted. Glancing at Jean, he smiled thinly, revealing perfectly white teeth, one of which, in the front, had a gold filling.

'My aunt won't bite,' Jean said quietly and, smiling, went across to the hall door, pulling it fully open.

'Unlike the aforementioned wolves,' she heard Uncle Fergus mutter in an unsteady voice. Christopher came rushing into the room and moved across to his uncle's side, taking his arm.

'This is Aunt Elizabeth,' he said, his face slightly flushed. Aunt Dizzy stepped grandly into the room, her hand outstretched, tinted teeth plainly visible within her smile.

'*So* lovely to meet you, Mr . . . Shall I call you Fergus? Uncle? Or both? What an *interesting* suit. Christopher has been telling me all about you. When we weren't arguing about wolves. I am utterly exhausted. Really, Jean, we walked along the south boundary of the zoo and I was aggrieved. Those poor creatures, so confined. In this day and age. Is tea ready? Are we going upstairs? Has Freida come? You may take my arm, Christopher's Uncle Fergus. I am a little at odds with the stairs. My damned niece *still* hasn't done anything about it. She's obstinate.'

'I am rewardingly charmed to meet you, rewardingly charmed,' Uncle Fergus said rather vaguely, still looking ill at ease.

'*Are* you?' Aunt Dizzy responded, putting her arm through his. 'Shall we ascend to the drawing-room for tea? Christopher has organized everything. A sumptuous spread. I'm bloody starving.'

•

'They won't stop *talking*,' Christopher said urgently to Jean. He had followed her downstairs, an hour later, into the kitchen where she was preparing more tea and hurriedly slicing cucumber. 'They're ignoring me, as if I wasn't there.'

Jean laughed. 'Then that simply means the afternoon is a success. Now stop wringing your hands and worrying. Aunt Dizzy knows about you and your uncle. Is that what's upset you? I had a chat to her days ago. She is quite unfazed. In fact she thinks it's lovely for you to have someone, as she put it, to share intimacy with. *She* had girlfriends when she was young.'

'You shouldn't have told her.'

'Well, I did.'

Christopher remained silent for a moment, staring at the kettle which was about to boil. Then he took up a knife and began to butter bread.

'You mean like Freida?' he asked.

'Oh yes. Men friends too. She was quite the raver. A long time ago, now.'

'We don't . . . you know . . . *do* anything, Uncle and me.'

'You mean sleep together?'

Christopher's face went bright scarlet.

'Uncle Fergus won't. Not until I'm older. He said that we should really be married before anything like that should happen, anyway.'

'But . . .' Jean glanced at Christopher and then looked away. His face was rigid with embarrassment. She didn't continue with the unnecessary, obvious comment that men couldn't marry.

'He's really moral,' said Christopher. 'Mother probably thinks that's all he wants, you know . . .'

'Sex?'

Christopher nodded. He handed her slices of buttered bread but wouldn't look up at her.

'*Sex*,' he whispered. '*She* wouldn't use that word.'

'You mustn't be scared of it, Christopher,' Jean said, softly. He stopped buttering bread when she gestured that there were enough slices and stood with his arms at his sides looking warily at her out of the corner of his sight. His lips sagged.

'Did your parents ever talk to you? Your father?'

Christopher visibly relaxed. 'Father gave me a brochure once, about a year ago. Never said anything. The brochure didn't say much. I know all *about* it. I'm not stupid. But I was never interested in anyone except Uncle. Not that way. Boys at college are all pillocks. They just make crude jokes. I like the girls better. They don't know that I'm . . . queer.'

'*I* prefer the word gay,' Jean said and smirked. Christopher began to snigger. Then he stopped and began coughing. He doubled over and Jean found herself patting his back and helping him to a chair. From upstairs she could hear laughter and then Aunt Dizzy's voice.

'Jean! Jean! Where have you got to? There are two old maids bloody dying of thirst up here!'

Uncle Fergus whinnied with laughter.

The afternoon tea went on until past six o'clock. Aunt Dizzy did not even excuse herself to indulge in her habitual afternoon nap. She and Uncle Fergus noisily discussed everything, from the recent onslaught of baby-carrying Romanian refugee women begging on the Underground to whether the only female Prime Minister in the country *had*, before her downfall, set the women's movement back fifty years. The latter was something Aunt Dizzy was convinced of. 'Just as I am convinced, Jean, that I should be allowed to keep my room upstairs,' she remarked sharply.

Jean and Christopher sat mostly in silence, Christopher staring at his uncle with an expression of deep devotion. He clung on to Uncle Fergus's every word, glancing at Jean and Aunt Dizzy as if his uncle was speaking the whole truth and nothing but the truth in everything he said. The two of them sat close together on a sofa, evidently relaxed enough to hold hands. Uncle Fergus kept crossing then uncrossing his legs. He was wearing yellow socks and highly polished patent-leather black shoes. He'd consumed almost an entire plate of cucumber sandwiches by himself and giggled in a high-pitched, whinnying voice when he wasn't expounding on the world as he saw it.

'Of course things were a whole lot different when I was a lass,' Aunt Dizzy was saying. 'Nothing was spoken of. It was all perfectly bobbity-boo so long as nobody said anything. That's changed, thank the fates. And fighting back. I've thoroughly enjoyed all this outing that goes on nowadays. Demonstrations inside churches. Good for them. There's a pile of hypocritical rot in this country about sexual matters. One or two of those obnoxious old hags in the Lords should be taken across to the green and stripped before being shot.' Then she turned towards Jean and asked, 'Is Freida not coming? I thought you said she was coming?' but without waiting for a reply went on to relate an event in her past at a garden party, where she fell in love with one of the maids, despite just having got engaged to Freddie Braymount the week before, who later married an earl's daughter and disgraced his entire family with his unquenchable thirst for little girls and pornographic photographs, all of which was exposed in the press. 'He's gone now,' she added. 'Shot himself in the head back in 1978. Times aren't what they used to be. Far too little scandal, everything's hushed up and no one has any shame.'

Uncle Fergus and Christopher sat entwining their fingers together. Both, Jean noticed, wore gold bands on the third finger of their left hands. She had noticed Christopher's before, but he had never mentioned anything about it and neither had she. The telephone rang downstairs, just as Uncle Fergus was explaining that he had to leave. There was a function to attend, to which Christopher was unfortunately not invited.

'Discretion still has to be observed,' he said.

'Well, I was going to suggest dinner and a round or two of Scrabble,' Aunt Dizzy said to him without even glancing Jean's way. 'Never mind, I'm sure you'll be here again. I'll have to fall back on the lad.'

Christopher had begun to tell her about some theatrical connections Uncle Fergus possessed as Jean left the room.

There was a lengthy silence when she answered the telephone.

'It's Will,' came William's voice. 'Hello, Jean.'

'William. I did mean to call you,' Jean responded. 'I received your note. You're at the Connaught?'

'Just for a day or so, then back to New York. How are you, Jean? I thought you might have at least called me.'

Laughter drifted down from upstairs. Aunt Dizzy cried out, 'Whoop-whoop! Whoop-whoop!' and something heavy crashed to the floor.

'Frieda saw you at the theatre a short while ago,' Jean said hastily, feeling inadequate and trying to think of something more interesting to say. She sounded inane. 'So I knew you were back.'

'I did notice. Few missed seeing her. She should have come over. I wasn't so impressed by the look of her . . . companion.'

'Mandy someone. Wants to move in.'

'Look, Jean. Why I've called. I need to come and see you. I won't insist, but it's something I don't wish to speak about over the phone. Would it be convenient?'

Shades of Mr Alder, Jean thought. 'Oh dear, let me think.

Well, all right. I've Aunt Dizzy living here now. Don't ask. Chr . . . someone's taking her out for the morning. What about ten-thirtyish, coffee?'

'I could take you out, an early lunch.'

'No, you come here. I'd prefer it.'

'Well, if you're sure. So, how are you?'

There were voices behind her coming down the stairs and into the morning-room.

'. . . and I really didn't mind about her broken, chipped dentures at all,' Aunt Dizzy was saying. 'They didn't hurt.'

Uncle Fergus was whinnying.

'Look, I'm sorry,' Jean said hurriedly into the receiver. 'I've company. I'd best go. I'll see you tomorrow,' and before William could respond she replaced the receiver, turning and smiling as Uncle Fergus made his way towards her, right hand outstretched, gold-filled tooth exposed in a rictus smile.

'What a splendiferous afternoon, Jean Barrie,' he was saying. 'Your aunt is jollity personified. Utter contagion. I do hope I shall not be construed as being impertinent, I fear I ignored you in favour of dear Elizabeth. Now. As I said earlier, we must think on, about you both coming down to the country seat, very soon. I've not been down for weeks and I need the change. I'll let Christopher know the details of when, etcetera, eh?' and he took Jean's hand and pressed it delicately to his moustached lips, emitting a smacking sound, his eyes never leaving hers. Christopher was hovering in the background, wringing his hands. When Jean caught his eye he mouthed the words 'She wants to go to sleep', pointing upwards.

'It was an experience to meet you, Fergus,' Jean said. 'I'll leave you to say goodbye to each other. You are welcome to call any time. I mean that.'

•

Christopher, an hour later, was in the bath. Jean had delicately suggested that he take a bath at least once a day. He had complied quite happily. Aunt Dizzy was in her room resting. Exhausted, Jean had fallen asleep in an armchair in the morning-room. She had heard some noises but had not opened her eyes, thinking that it would be Christopher, and half lay, curled up in the chair, face turned towards the french windows. She had fallen into a deep sleep when she was awake again suddenly, realizing she had heard the front door being opened and closed several times. She'd been dreaming of William and her mother dancing together on the lawn, with a full orchestra somehow arranged in the background on a brightly lit podium. Freida had been singing a Cole Porter song out of tune at a microphone. She opened her eyes slowly. The house had grown quite dark and she had not switched on any lights. Yet she was certain there was a figure moving away from her along the hall when she turned to look. The hall door was open, whereas she had left it closed after Uncle Fergus had left. Jean shook her head, only half awake.

'Hello, is someone there?' she called out. There were hurried footsteps and the front door was opened. With little street light she could only see someone silhouetted in the doorway. 'Freida? Is that you?' There was no response. The figure moved swiftly out on to the steps, pulling the door closed. Jean struggled up out of the chair and switched on a lamp. The hall was empty. By the time she got to the front door, opened it and looked out all she could see over the privet hedge was the top half of a taxi moving fast away from the house.

Closing the door, switching on the hall lights, she immediately noticed the keys sitting on the hall table alongside a card.

Goodbye, Jean Barrie, she read aloud after picking up the

card, then the keys. *I will never, ever forget your kindness and your beauty. Catherine.*

Still clutching the keys, letting the card drop back on to the table, Jean retraced her steps into the morning-room and hurried up the stairs. As she passed Christopher's and Aunt Dizzy's shared bathroom she could hear the sound of splashing water and Christopher humming. A smell like bleach wafted in the air.

On the uppermost floor Catherine Truman's rooms were empty, apart from the furniture. There was a faint lingering odour of incense. The walls had some time been painted a gloss white, where they had been a dull brown when the Fallen Nun had moved in. There was almost no trace of anyone having been living there. Jean had never been into the rooms in all the time her lodger had been in the house. She had never wished to intrude.

On the small casual table in the main room sat one long-stemmed white rose, still fresh. There were droplets of water on the petals. Opposite, on the wall where once had been a fireplace, was painted from floor to ceiling an enormous portrait of a woman, reclining lasciviously in an armchair. The figure was naked. Jean stared at it for several minutes, her hands moving up to her mouth and remaining there, her heart beginning to thud uncomfortably. The painting was realistic, revealing, disturbingly realized in its detail.

Jean turned and hurried out, relocking the door behind her in a rush and almost running down the stairs. For the first time in a week she opened a bottle of gin once she reached the kitchen and downed two glasses before she sat nursing a third. As she'd stepped rapidly along the downstairs hall, trying not to think about anything, heading for the kitchen, something caused her to stop and stare. The framed poster of herself that Freida had once given her and which had promoted her second album was missing from the wall.

SEVEN

With Christopher's help Jean had managed, not without difficulty, to move Aunt Dizzy's new orthopaedic bed upstairs and carry the one she had been sleeping in down to the renovated reception room. Her card-table and two Queen Anne chairs had also been taken up to the first floor.

'You can stay upstairs now, Auntie,' Jean told her. 'I'll enquire about stair-lifts.'

'*Will* you?' Aunt Dizzy responded. Later, she said, 'I'm so *relieved* you've changed your mind, Jean. About the rooms. The one downstairs is all very well, but it looks like a hospital ward. Or a morgue. It lacks character. It's a man's room.'

She and Christopher had gone out in a taxi to visit an art exhibition at the Institute of Contemporary Art.

'It's a collection of nude transsexual poses,' Aunt Dizzy had explained over breakfast. 'Very explicit, I believe. Body-part art as never seen anywhere before in public.' She had come across an advertisement for it in a trendy listings magazine and thought the exhibition might be educational for Christopher. 'As for myself,' she added, as Jean hesitated over her warmed-milk cereal, 'I've seen nearly everything of the flesh in my day. You remember the maid I said I fell in love with, just after my engagement to Freddie Braymount? She was a man underneath her garb. Quite a shock, I tell you, when she disrobed. It thoroughly confused everyone at the time. After the truth also came out, so to speak,' she went on, laughing loudly, 'the family got rid of the poor soul and I faced the ignominy of being engaged for two months to a pervert. Life is too quiet now, Jean. Boring. I do think you should telephone the police about the stolen poster. Stir things up a little. The pot of life is becoming a trifle stagnant.' Christopher, standing at the sink, sniggered.

William was expected in less than half an hour. Jean abandoned her usual dress code of loose cotton trousers and plain sweatshirt which she wore about the house for a long-sleeved tasteful dress that made her look ten years older. She decided that a mumsy, prim look would be better. William, she felt certain, would have the good manners to come alone. She had wondered momentarily what it was he might want. Money did not seem likely. The deeds to Acacia Road were in her name. The past, if not assimilated, was at least never mentioned any longer. There was no possible reason for William, or herself, to seek reconciliation.

She again tried to telephone Freida. Now there appeared to be a fault on the line that British Telecom, for all its computer wisdom, could tell her nothing about.

'There's a fault on the line,' she was cheerfully informed when she enquired. When she asked politely for an explanation the same obvious statement was repeated before it was suggested that Jean have a nice day. The chirpy female voice had squawked with an American accent.

Jean had not seen William for over a year. They had been in touch by letter or between solicitors. The divorce had been agonizingly slow to reach a decree absolute but amicable enough under the circumstances. For most of the time William had remained in New York, where he had fled to. He'd allegedly done well there, possessed offices in Manhattan and two secretaries, one of whom was from Birmingham and who had known his mother, a fact related by letter that caused Jean inexplicably to laugh.

He arrived at exactly ten thirty. Jean let him wait at the front door for at least two minutes while she sat in the morning-room, the french windows open to the crisp morning air, breathing deeply and practising an air of indifference by making facial expressions that had more to do with nervous tics into a hand mirror. She decided at the last moment that artifice would not do. She would simply be herself, if that were possible. William, however, who had for so long been confrontational, defensive and inclined towards verbal aggression, was about to surprise her. Uncharacteristically he smiled warmly when she opened the door. He had brought her a tasteful arrangement of camellias and fern fronds, expensively wrapped.

'Hello, Lady Jean,' he said in a low voice that, like his smile, also exuded warmth. Before she could pull back he leant forward and delicately planted a kiss on her cheek that did not quite connect. She allowed him to step past and followed him along the hall, examining him from behind. He had not put on an ounce of extra weight and wore an expensive suit with a haircut to match. He was lightly tanned, his eyes clear and sharp. For a moment a pang of nostalgia bit into her which she managed to suppress. He stopped short at the large gap on the hall wall, turning to glance at her with a raised eyebrow.

'I'm having it reframed,' she said quickly. 'The glass broke completely. Thank you for noticing.'

Jean had closed the doors along the hall. William moved confidently through into the morning-room, standing there smiling at her, handing over the flowers then peering out through the french windows as all visitors did, the room so dark, the garden so spring-bright.

'Everything looks healthy,' he commented, referring, she assumed, to the garden.

'I have someone who takes care of it,' she told him. 'Would you like coffee now or later?'

'Now would be perfect. May I sit down?'

William sat before she could reply. She stepped past him to take the flowers into the kitchen. With no vase at hand to put them in – Uncle Fergus's contribution sat elegantly in her bedroom – she ran water into one of the sinks and left them there in order to attend to the coffee. She did not return to the morning-room until the coffee was ready and on a tray, listening for any sounds but hearing nothing. William was examining one of her reissued collections on CD when she rejoined him. She had deliberately left a pile of them where he would be bound to notice. He glanced up and smiled.

'Doing well?' he asked, angling the CD towards her. She nodded.

'As far as I know. What is it you want, William?'

She knew straight away from his expression that she'd been too abrupt or even rude, but the words slipped out and she winced. Old habits died hard. He stared across at her and smiled again, a little sadly, she thought. For a moment an image of Anthony Hibbert came to mind. The image rather checked her. Anthony Hibbert looked a little like William when *he* had been in his twenties.

'The coffee smells delicious,' he said.

'There's a new deli up in the high street. Chr ... someone gets it for me. Milk, sugar? I can't remember,' Jean asked and then began to laugh. William stared at the CD, then carefully placed it back on the pile.

Eventually he told her a little about New York. Still speaking in a low, modulated voice, he did not sound like the William she remembered. He had been prone, in the last months of their marriage, to shout at her. Jean had been a fucking cold, irresponsible and mean bitch. There had been other endearments which descended into true obscenity, communicated on an almost daily basis. Now he sat across from her looking relaxed, fit, behaving with easy grace. His eyes revealed nothing but warmth, as if the two of them had always been casual, respectful friends.

'What about you?' he finally asked.

'Oh well. Aunt Dizzy's here now. Living here. Almost a mutual agreement. She won't have aged that much since you last saw her, but she's more forgetful. Contrary but hardly fragile. She's become quite energetic. In fact she's out almost every day, with Chr . . . With Christopher. He lives here with me, too', and when William said nothing but stared at her with a slightly uncertain, quizzical gaze she added, 'Oh, nothing like that. Christopher's seventeen. He's a student. Takes care of the garden. He cooks. Fetches and carries. He had troubles at home. Aunt Dizzy adores him.'

'Same old Jean. Champion of the weak.'

She stared back at him coolly and smiled.

'Did I hear you are going to publish a biography?' William asked.

'Autobiography. There were plans. I came to the conclusion that I really had no interest in one at all. I had nothing to say. It just . . . lapsed. I made a few tapes for someone. Wrote notes. I didn't enjoy it. The publisher offered a small fortune in a syco-phantic way.'

'But.'

'Yes, but. You look well. New York agrees with you?'

'Yes and no. I do miss London. The two places aren't compar-able.'

They were sipping the last of the coffee, had talked of incon-sequential topics such as weather and theatre and the change of government, when William suddenly got up from his chair and went to stand at the french windows with his back to her. Two collared doves flew up into the pale sky from the lawn.

'I came to see you about Father,' he said gently. For a second his shoulders shook and he bowed his head. Then he straightened, coughed and returned to his chair, leaning forward in it and resting his elbows on his knees. His eyes were quite dry.

'He's got himself into a bit of a state,' William said. 'He hadn't told me. You know how uncomplaining he always was. I went down to Brighton, just after I flew over.'

'Hove, actually,' Jean said into the following long silence, but William did not even smile. He went on as if she had not spoken at all.

'Father claims he had to sell the house. Numerous unpaid debts, large ones. He somehow owed a small fortune in back Community Charges he'd ignored. Insurances he let lapse didn't cover anything. He then had to have a couple of operations, refused to go on a waiting-list and went private. To do with his legs. He even spent time in a wheelchair. Where he was living – I knew he'd changed his address but I'd no idea what it was he'd moved to – well, he'd lied about it. I found him in a squalid bedsit, in a grimy little street near the end of Western Road. Living off benefits. All his savings are gone. The place is – was – an utter disgrace. Not entirely his own making. He was doing the best he could, too proud, too obstinate to tell me. He wrote a few times to New York. Never said a word about any difficulty. Just that he'd decided to sell the old house and buy something central. I've moved him into a hotel for the interim. Along the front. Saw he was comfortable, paid for all he needed in advance where I could and wrote him a cheque. It isn't the money that's the problem. I really don't know what to do about him. I wondered . . . I was hoping you might go down to visit.

He kept asking about you in his letters, didn't wish to intrude and contact you. His circumstances all happened rather suddenly. So he said.'

'Of course. Of *course* I'll go down. Oh Lord. And you honestly had no idea? No inkling at all?'

'No. He sent cheerful cards and notes to New York, seemed contented, still missing Mother of course. I really had no forewarning. I gather he assumed I was so settled in New York that I wouldn't be back. I just turned up, which displeased him immensely. It all rather shocked me.'

'Couldn't you tell from the address? Something, surely?' Jean asked.

William shook his head.

'He was being devious. Lying about everything so as not to worry me. I really did believe he'd bought a smaller house and he was pleased with it. He wrote nothing about his illness.'

'Which was?'

'Oh, blocked arteries in his legs. Extremely bad circulation. He said he almost lost one of the legs. All those years smoking. They managed to save both legs, but he can't walk as far as he wants to, as he used to. The operations were formidably expensive. It was those that cleaned him out, I suspect. Had one of those electric chairs for some time, bought it second-hand. Kept it under a cover on his doorstep. It was still there. A ground floor bedsit, easy access to the street. One room barely furnished. Ripped wallpaper. Really squalid, Jean. The room smelt.'

'Poor Ivan!'

'You know, the most upsetting part of it was that he seemed quite resigned to living like that. Said it was all he needed, that with Mother gone he never minded where he'd live. He'd neglected himself. Some sort of social worker turned up while I was there. Treated him with barely concealed casual contempt. I told her to leave. I moved him out the same day. He tried to hide his gratitude with bluster, but I know he was enormously relieved.'

'When do you go back? To New York?'

'I *have* to be back by tomorrow evening at the latest. I thought I'd arrange some time off, spend time with him. Get him settled somewhere. There's no one else. He's refused to join me in New York. He doesn't appear to have any friends down there. He doesn't like the idea of a hotel. In fact he hates it.'

'I'll go tomorrow, I've just decided. There's no reason I shouldn't go down straight away. Which hotel?'

'The Thistle, on the front. I suggested the Grand. Too pretentious, he said. He would love to see you, Jean. He may never have shown it, but he was rather fond of you. Too unable to say, while Mother was alive.'

'Understandable.'

William stared down at his hands, examining his fingers as if he had never seen them before. He glanced up at her and looked away.

'Mother spoke of you just before she died. She regretted never having got to know you better. That she'd judged you harshly. All those years. I was with her the morning she went. She sat there in bed wearing a new bedjacket I'd bought her. Got into a panic that it was buttoned incorrectly. She didn't want to be laughed at by the nurses. They'd been treating her as if she were a child. She prattled on. After a while she lay back quietly, smiling at me. Then she closed her eyes and in a moment she was gone. I thought she'd gone to sleep.'

William sat staring down at the floor. Jean had an urge to lean forward, to reach out, but stayed where she was. William was genuinely close to tears.

He stayed for less than an hour. Jean guessed that he did not wish to encounter Aunt Dizzy. He wrote the details of the hotel on a slip of paper, along with his mobile-phone number.

'Look, I'll call you from New York to let you know when I'll be back. I can't avoid a couple of meetings, I did try to wangle my way out of them but . . .'

'I understand, really. I'll go down tomorrow morning. Take him out to lunch, whatever he might like.'

He turned to look at her as he went out the front door. She could see on his face that there was something more he wanted to say, but instead he carried on up into the street. She followed him as far as the gate and watched as he hurried towards the tube station. He didn't look back. He swung his arms and appeared to be gazing at the grey sky. The morning had turned cold; heavy cloud hung low. Jean shivered and went back into the house.

'Utterly disgraceful behaviour if you ask me,' Jean heard Aunt Dizzy say as she came in the door. Jean was in the front reception room, sitting on the bed, deep in thought. 'I should have been rude, just out of spite. I'm sorry, Christopher, but your damned mother is a foul-mouthed fishwife who doesn't deserve you. You're a fine lad, even if you are an ugly duck.'

Jean remained where she was, but Aunt Dizzy, noticing her as she passed, swept into the room and stood with legs apart clutching her handbag to her sagging bosom. The jacket of her pale-lemon dress-suit was wrinkled. Her face was a study of indignation.

'I am livid, Jean. We ran into Christopher's mother in the high street and she treated him to what I can only describe as verbal abuse. Ignored me. Right there, with people watching! She began by shouting that the Devil had claimed him now and he was damned to unhappiness and eventually to Hell. I could have swiped at her. It didn't help when Christopher began crying. We've bought lunch. He's gone to prepare it. Nut cutlets and a selection of French mushrooms. I'm bloody starving. Good exhibition. Fascinating. You might have enjoyed it. So what have you been up to? Nothing, I expect. Mooning about.'

Jean had not told Aunt Dizzy about William's planned visit. There had never been any form of affection between the two.

'I told Christopher, cry and you lose a barrel of salt. Laugh and the world respects you. The poor lamb was in a dreadful state after his mother flounced off. She has victimized him for years, it seems. There is no accounting for a son's love.'

After Aunt Dizzy had gone upstairs to freshen up, Jean tried to call Freida again. The line having apparently been repaired, the telephone rang and went on ringing. Jean was about to replace the receiver when someone answered.

'May I please speak to Freida?' Jean asked. The voice sounded nothing like Mandy's but she was not sure that it wasn't her.

'Who?'

'Freida. Freida Weinreb. Who am I talking to?'

There was a mumbled response, then the receiver was clunked down. In the background Jean heard several voices and then laughter. The receiver was picked up and unceremoniously put back into its cradle. Jean tried again. This time she received the engaged tone.

Christopher had stepped into the hall and was staring at her. He offered a thin smile. His eyes were swollen and red. His lips sagged.

'Lunch,' he said. 'Nut cutlets, onions, mushrooms. I'll make coffee. Who brought the flowers?'

Jean replaced the receiver.

'No one. I mean . . . I did. Bought them. Christopher, are you all right?'

Christopher shrugged. He began to wring his hands. Jean had a sudden urge to shout at him, just as his mother evidently had. She felt angry and irritable but could not take it out on him. It was William she wanted to shout at. Christopher turned away and she followed him through into the kitchen. There was a scratching sound in the walls.

'Rats,' she muttered. 'Bloody sodding rats.'

EIGHT

The Brighton train was almost full. Jean sat beside a woman in a full-length white leather coat who kept sucking her teeth and scratching one of her over-large purple-veined legs. She glanced at Jean as she sat down as if a piece of over-ripe dog poop was attached to Jean's shoe. Jean smiled politely. She regretted not buying a first-class ticket.

She had left the house early, leaving a note sitting on the breakfast table in the kitchen, written in large letters. *GONE SOUTH. DAY OUT. TAKE CARE. LOVE, EARTH MOTHER.* Aunt Dizzy had kept Christopher up until gone one o'clock playing Scrabble in her room. Jean had lain in bed listening to their arguments and laughter, worrying about Freida, then about the missing poster. It seemed obvious that Catherine Truman had taken the poster. It was hardly a collector's item, but it was signed – Freida had insisted – and Jean had remained, however uninterested she had become in her abandoned career, hugely popular. 'LADY POPJAZZ', had been a recent headline in a music magazine. Jean had appeared on the cover 'She truly connected the specialist world of jazz to popular soul.' The author of the piece had written at length, which Jean didn't mind as she was judged solely on her work and not on her character or her past or her looks or how she behaved in public, which is what mainly appeared to matter elsewhere when it came to success. It did irritate her a little that she was written about as if she didn't exist any longer. There had been no mention in the article about an autobiography. There *had* been talk at the publisher of her touring 'marketable points of reference' when her autobiography was launched. Appearing here, appearing there. Flying to America, Australia, even Japan, where her popularity was increasing. Not once was it mentioned that she would *sing*. There was a heated discussion over what she should wear and say, especially about her private, harrowing past.

The woman in the white leather coat got up and moved somewhere else a half-hour out from Victoria. Jean was able to move into the window seat and relax, clearing her mind by peering into rear gardens and at the occasional meadow. By the time the train pulled into Brighton she was even looking forward to the visit to a town she had, in the past, begun to enjoy. The mixture of sleaze and old grandeur, the busy, traffic-choked streets were hardly a complete change from London until the stroll down Queens Road eventually revealed the endless expanse of the sea. She had considered, numerous times, selling Acacia Road and moving down to Brighton. The children had wanted to do just that, years ago. It was a little dream that she'd told no one about, even Freida. The dream comforted, as it had remained simply a small fantasy which could be made to come true with not a great amount of effort or sacrifice. The dream had, at times, been vivid. It comforted her the most after William had walked out of her life.

The morning was clear and slightly chilled as she made her way out through the station and across into Queens Road. There were large signs announcing a complete renovation of the area, which somehow depressed her. Brighton, like London, did not invite change. Though tempted to turn off, once she reached and crossed the North Street junction, to visit Duke Street, she kept on down to King's Road and to the sea, crossing the busy, noisy front to stand on the promenade, leaning on the familiar pale-blue railings. She gazed to her right towards the partly restored but still derelict West Pier, breathing in deeply the pungent odour of the sea in front of her, gazing upwards at the sky. She *could* live down here, she thought. People passing, in groups or alone, walked in a relaxed manner. Two long trails of teenage European students streamed by in different directions, some wearing backpacks, chattering loudly. An elderly couple sat on a bench eating steaming chips with wooden forks. Below, a young woman with bright red hair, wearing green tights and a yellow top, was doing balletic aerobics on the puce-coloured pebbles. To the left, yards away, workmen were removing a tarpaulin from an ancient merry-go-round Jean had not remembered seeing before.

The hotel was not far from where she'd emerged on to the seafront. She almost passed it as she walked, deep in thoughts of leaving London altogether and perhaps buying one of the small terraced houses in one of the streets off Madeira Drive. She sauntered, hands in the pockets of her woollen coat, aware of people occasionally glancing her way with incurious eyes. For a moment she stood outside the hotel staring up at its green-glass frontage, now a little reluctant to enter, when the Brighton streets and familiar places tempted her to spend the day in nostalgic self indulgence. A little window-shopping in the Lanes, a visit to the museum, perhaps a taxi down to the Marina for afternoon tea before heading home. It was a perfect day for walking. Yet she dutifully went up the steps and into the hotel foyer, briskly heading across to the reception desk. A youngish woman with thin lips smiled sweetly when Jean asked for Ivan Fitzpatrick. She studied the ubiquitous computer and then began to frown.

'Sorry, there's no one of that name registered,' she said eventually. 'Fitzpatrick. No, doesn't look like it. Have you got the right hotel? Oh, hang on. Sorry. We *did* have a Mr Fitzpatrick, yes, Ivan, staying here, but he suddenly booked himself out yesterday afternoon. I remember now. Sorry. There was a problem of overpayment. Whoops, shouldn't have said that!'

'Did he leave a forwarding address?'

'Not . . . that I know of. He might have signed the visitors' book. Just a moment.'

The woman disappeared into a back room but returned almost immediately.

'Here we are. Now, let's have a look.'

Jean glanced around the reception area. It seemed a very bright and cheerful hotel. A few people were sitting about on sofas and chairs sipping tea or coffee. It was quiet. Sunlight streamed across the floor, green-tinged from the window glass.

'All he put was Farm Road, Brighton. But I think that's in Hove . . . No proper address. I don't suppose I should have told you that either! But do I care? I've just handed in my notice.'

'Thank you so much,' Jean responded and smiled as warmly as she could. She was aware of the young woman's appraising gaze before she turned and headed swiftly back out on to the street.

Farm Road was somewhere along towards the end of Western Road, just before Palmeira Square, Jean vaguely recalled. She had walked along that way numerous times with the children, looking out for blue plaques – Winston Churchill went to school somewhere near Farm Road – heading for the indoor swimming-pool, in the days when Brighton had become as familiar to her as the streets of St John's Wood. She had walked for miles, it seemed, back then. Jared had nagged for them to move down, just so he could be closer to her parents. He had adored her father to the point of idolatry.

She took a circuitous route, not wishing to retrace the streets she had once walked along, Gemma and Jared holding her hands and urging her onwards. It seemed, also, that William had never been with them on those treks, that it had only ever been her and the children. She walked at a quickened pace, along the front, past the paddling-pool, the empty and abandoned boating-pool to Brunswick lawns and across the road, up through the square, emerging again into Western Road. She could see the Farm Road street sign down to her left. She stood opposite for some time, uncertain about going on. The morning had grown warmer, though the sunlight was thin. She was tempted to turn back, to sit for a while in Brunswick Square. Was it *necessary* to visit William's father? She had never been close to him. Why had she so readily and without thought told William she would visit? What on earth would she find to say?

The street was narrow in parts and not inviting. She would walk up it, then back and then decide what to do. There was no one about as she moved into it, the time of morning before the lunch-hour when local people had already walked dogs and were now at work or indoors. So she noticed the lone figure sitting on the front steps of a rather decrepit-looking building straight away and paused, trying to decide if she should cross and ask him if he knew where Ivan Fitzpatrick lived. Hardly likely, she supposed. Then the man stood up. He went to turn, to go inside. He stared straight at her and over his gaunt, pale face grew a slow smile of recognition. He'd been smoking a cigarette which he flicked out into the gutter and then stood gazing at her. He nodded once but did not speak. Jean tentatively crossed the road, not looking at him as she did so but watching for traffic.

'William said you might come down. Here you are. I've been watching for you.'

'Hello, Ivan. I'd no idea of your address . . .'

'Oh, I sit out here a lot, you know. Passing the time. It's growing warmer. You went to the hotel?'

Jean nodded. Her former father-in-law did not look well. He was far thinner than she remembered, as well as much older. He wore a pair of faded, loose-fitting jeans and his hair was unbrushed. She had never seen him out of a suit before. He had dressed immaculately, even on holiday. She and William had spent one long weekend with Ivan and May in Suffolk before the children were born. It had not been an enjoyable weekend. Ivan Fitzpatrick had worn a suit even on the walks they'd taken along grassy lanes beside the flat grey sea. Very little had been said and he'd acted morose, even distant. May Fitzpatrick had spent most of the weekend with pursed lips and wearing a disapproving smile when she hadn't been rummaging in her handbag or complaining about the hotel they'd stayed in.

'Would you like to come in? A cup of tea? I can just about manage that,' Ivan asked her in a neutral tone. She followed him up the steps and through the open door into a dingy and dark hallway. At the far end were uncarpeted stairs. The walls were bare. An old bicycle was propped upside-down, a wheel missing. Ivan turned and pushed open a door to his right.

'Home,' he said. 'Don't be alarmed. Don't expect much. I *have* tidied up a little. William thought you'd find me at the hotel. Still thinks so, no doubt. He'll be gone now. Back to New York. Sit yourself down. The chair's clean. I'll rummage for tea bags.'

The room was rather large with a high ceiling yellow from years of cooking and smoke and neglect. There was a bed covered by a patterned continental quilt, a table and chairs, one armchair. In a corner stood a cheap fitted unit on which sat a microwave and a gas ring. Opposite was a built-in wash-basin.

'Bathroom's along the hall if you need it. Long walk from the hotel. I'm surprised you bothered, quite frankly. No, that sounds rude. The problem of living alone.' Ivan attempted to light the gas ring, which was old and basic. Jean quickly looked away and winced as Ivan lit a second match. She moved to sit on one of the hard wooden chairs at the table. The room was warm. The carpet looked new. She gazed curiously at a small framed Constable print hanging crookedly above the bed.

'I decided to come back,' Ivan told her, 'as I couldn't stand the hotel. Too impersonal. Fortunately this place is still mine. William rushed me out of it as if the building was about to collapse, so I went along without protest, just to make him feel he was doing something worthy, as my son. After one night in the hotel I simply returned. I don't mind it here. Pleasant landlord. Lives a few doors away. Decent sort. His wife fusses over me, lets me use the machines at the launderette for free as she works there. Brings down the occasional meal.' He turned and smiled at her. 'How the mighty have fallen, Jean. I know what you'll be thinking. Old age has brought many changes. Without May, life is not beautiful.'

'You should have contacted me when she died,' Jean said quietly. 'I could have helped. In some way. William never bothered to let me know at the time.'

Ivan shrugged but didn't immediately respond. Carefully he poured boiling water into two mugs, then dropped in tea bags from an opened box. He spooned in milk powder. There was no refrigerator in the room.

'You had enough to contend with yourself, Jean. Didn't wish to burden you. I thought of it. I've coped. Mostly. I've started to talk to her recently, you know. To May. I natter on about my days. I have her ashes, hidden away. It helps, talking to her. Loony tunes, perhaps.'

He carried the two mugs of tea across to the table and sat

down opposite, pushing one of them over to her. He took a sip of his tea and sighed.

'It was decent of you to come down. You needn't stay if you don't wish to. I'm sure it was your own idea, to visit. William bluffed about it, said he'd insist, that you had little better to do and would appreciate the outing. He was always a patronizing bastard even when he was young.'

'I'd rather like to take you out to lunch.'

Ivan stared back at her. From his shirt pocket he took out a tobacco tin and matches and began to roll a cigarette.

'How's the singing going?' he asked. 'William's told me nothing about you. How you've been faring. She's OK, he'd say. She's still up there living in that house. He never took to the idea of it being solely yours.'

'I don't sing any longer, Ivan,' Jean replied. 'Not in public. That's all over with. I gave up completely, after . . .' She fell silent and stared down at her mug. 'I thought you knew.'

'I'm sorry. Shouldn't pry. Don't, normally. You know, May talked about writing to you, before she was diagnosed, before the illness set in. She felt some need after the grandchildren . . . well, you know. Never told me what she wanted to say. She never did write as far as I gathered. May had a lot of regrets in her life and never did anything about any of them. She found relating to people very difficult. She was . . .' he stopped speaking and lit the rolled cigarette. Jean looked up and watched him. His face contracted and he opened and closed his mouth as if a sudden memory gave him pain. His hands shook as he reached up to wipe one of them across his eyes. Then he hung his head.

'You've caught me at a low ebb, Jean. I am sorry. It's the loneliness. It eats at you.' He spoke so quietly that Jean had to lean forward to hear. 'Day after day. It's like an unremarked disease for which there's no cure. I sit out there on those steps on fine days for hours. Sometimes I imagine I can see May walking up towards me. It's never her, of course. Always someone else. A stranger. One of them might nod as she passes by. A lot of widows living down here, Jean. Living out their lives in much the same way I live out mine. I walk, for miles some days. There and back, to see how far it is. Right down to the marina and back or along to the lagoon. Rarely speak to anyone. You become invisible when you reach a certain age. That's the one thing you notice. That you're invisible.'

After the speech he leant back in his chair and sipped tea and smoked. He looked exhausted and suddenly embarrassed. He glanced at her, then away.

'I used to walk a lot near here with the children, when they were small,' Jean said. 'There's a plaque, just across from the end of your street, somewhere there. Winston Churchill went to school close by.'

Ivan did not answer, but he nodded.

'I've been worried about Freida,' Jean went on. 'You remember my friend Freida? Freida Weinreb.'

Ivan suddenly sat forward and grinned. It was obviously an effort.

'Of course. Freida. How could anyone forget meeting her. May disliked her, but then she was never a good judge of anyone. Is she ill?'

'No, no, nothing like that. Well, I suppose she's disappeared. I can't get hold of her. Every time I call, the phone's either out of order or some stranger answers. It's been quite a while. It's the first time she's ever failed to appear, annoying me every few days. We're very close. What does one do when a friend goes missing? Call the police?'

Ivan shook his head. He turned slightly, stubbing out his cigarette and gazed fully at her, smiling.

'Gone away? Off to Paris? You told me once that she always flies off to Paris when she's fed up. Spends money with no regard to self-control.'

Jean stared at him.

'Fancy remembering that. Paris. Of course. You're probably right. Freida wasn't happy, about something. Someone. Why hadn't I thought of it myself? Thank you, Ivan. I have been rather distracted lately. Aunt Elizabeth lives with me now and a young man I've taken pity on. He's only seventeen and was thrown out of his parents' home. At seventeen!'

Ivan looked at her with his smile still in place, but his eyes had grown cool and they'd narrowed.

'You didn't have to do this, you know,' he said. 'Come down to cheer me up. Try to distract me so obviously. It's a little patronizing. We don't owe each other a thing.'

'Well, I'm here. I wanted to come. Really.'

'I'm sorry. Please forgive me. As I said, not a good day. Let me take *you* out to lunch. We'll go to Browns. Not far away. Excellent restaurant. Very . . . *English*. There isn't enough made of being English these days. I'll get changed and we can stroll along. I've a couple of suits left. You know, I found this shop, down the other end of Brighton. Jewish owner. Place is chock-full of suits and jackets and hats for gentlemen. All in perfect order. Extraordinary. I sold . . . But I digress. William condescended to give me some pocket money. We shall enjoy a glorious *English* lunch together and then you can go back up to town in the happy knowledge that you've done your duty. I shall report favourably. There, all settled.'

'There's a lot we could catch up on,' Jean suggested.

Ivan shook his head. 'No. I wouldn't say that. We'll just pass the time pleasantly. I'd enjoy that more.'

'William didn't say anything outright, but I did sense he was hoping I'd come down and sort you out.' Jean tried not to smile but failed.

Ivan laughed. 'My son was always a prat, Jean. Now there's a grand word. He married above his station, I always knew that. Told him so once and he stared at me as if I was barmy. Didn't understand. I suspected he had designs on your house. Secret designs. He *was* greedy. He should have been born much later, grown up amidst Thatcherite greed. Then he may well have become one of the monsters that that time produced. As it is, he was too weak to succeed in such a direction. Fortunately. Did he tell you he would be back?'

Jean nodded.

'Thought so. He won't be. He will have realized there's little in it for him. He'll decide that he's done his bit. He did love you, Jean. He loved you deeply. I should give him credit for that. But when the chips were down he fled. I let him book me into the hotel just to make him to feel he was helping. I had no intention of staying there. To be perfectly honest, I hate living here, too, but there you have it. Life without May.'

He fell silent.

Jean waited outside the house in the sunlight while Ivan shaved and changed clothes. She watched a tiny woman in a filthy, grossly stained blue overcoat and plimsolls wandering down Farm Road on the opposite pavement with an equally tiny dog attached to a length of string. The dog kept barking shrilly at nothing in particular. The woman stopped to examine the contents of a rubbish bin. Her hair was damp or greasy and so thin that her scalp showed through. There were whiskers growing from her chin. She was still in sight when Ivan appeared, in suit and overcoat, hair combed, face flushed and smooth.

'Now *she's* a real character,' he told her. 'Lives in the next

street, always about. Talks eloquently about religion and litera-
ture. Calls her dog Persephone. Speaks to everyone, but most
shy away as she smells. Had many a long chat to her. She lived in
India for most of her life. Knew a maharajah. Intimately, she told
me. Keeps advising me to get a small dog and to *talk* to people.
She sometimes breaks into song as she wanders about. Seems
perfectly happy with her lot in life. I rather envy her.'

Over a lunch of braised lamb chops and perfectly steamed veg-
etables, followed by an old-fashioned steamed pudding, Ivan
did tell her a little about his days, despite having rejected Jean's
suggestion that they might catch up. What impressed itself on
her was that, away from his room, he was cheerfully pragmatic
about his loneliness, not seeking sympathy but talking about it
as if he was describing someone else, in an ironic manner that
warmed her to him. The routine, the tiny details were entertaining because they were related with a certain resigned humour.
He did grow close to tears twice, yet pulling back and silently
controlling what she could see as a fear of what might lie ahead.
Without his wife, without May. He could not stop bringing her
into the conversation. They talked, without pause, relaxed in
each other's company to an extent that almost surprised Jean.
He was nothing like William at all, in any way.

As they sipped perfectly brewed tea she looked across at him
and said gently, 'Why don't you come up to London for the rest
of the day. And evening. Or for a few days. A little break. Goodness knows I have the room. You could stay at the house. You'd
like my aunt. I think you met, once, long ago. Christopher's
fine, a little maudlin but fine. He's out most of the time. We
could visit a few places, galleries, whatever, have more lunches
out.'

Ivan stared down at his cup, running his finger around its

delicately thin rim. His face was unreadable. She thought he might have taken umbrage.

'I'd really like you to come up, Ivan. Just pack a bag. We can take a late afternoon train. There's no reason I can see to prevent it, is there?'

He raised his head and gazed at her. For a second his lips trembled slightly. He licked them.

'I'd like that very much,' he said almost in a whisper. 'I'd like that *very* much.'

'We'll not decide on any time limit,' Jean said quickly. 'Just come up with me, today. Take it from there.'

Jean insisted on paying for the lunch. Ivan acquiesced rather reluctantly and glanced about as if the only other couple there might notice and show disapproval. As they headed down to the front Jean put her arm through his.

'I almost didn't come to visit you at all, you know,' she said.

Ivan chuckled. 'And I wouldn't have blamed you one bit. Did you plan to ask me up to London? That is, if you had fully intended to visit?'

'No. Quite honestly I would rather have spent the day down here shopping. But one makes one's choices.'

They exchanged doleful grins then began to laugh.

'I'd rather William not be told, my dear. That I shall be staying with you.'

'I shan't say a word. My lips are sealed if he should call. I agree with you, I doubt that he will. Anyway, that's enough. Does this mean that you *will* stay up in London for a few days? A week perhaps?'

Ivan simply smiled and squeezed her arm.

'There we are,' he said, nodding forward. 'The brightling Brighton sea.'

Arm in arm they continued in the sunshine towards the Hove

lawns. The day had become warmer while they'd been having lunch, the colour of the sky deepening. Seagulls screeched from rooftops. There were more people about. Jean began to relate a little of Aunt Dizzy's behaviour while she had been living at the hotel in Mayfair. By the time they reached the promenade Ivan was chuckling. I *like* this man, Jean thought. It was almost as if she was out walking with someone she had just met, a stranger who was kind and courteous and gently ironic. If she was not careful she might end up having enjoyed a most pleasant day.

NINE

Two weeks had passed. Jean had still not heard from Freida. Her telephone rang unanswered. Ivan Fitzpatrick had settled into the third guest room on the first floor with apparent ease. There had been no mention of when he might return to Brighton. Jean had not asked. He acted as though he would remain for the duration. She had even been up into the attic to find some suits for him that had belonged to her father. It had not upset her, sorting through the trunks of clothing. She had expected it to. Not having wished to be rid of her parents' belongings, she had decided never to look at them ever again. Time had proved her wrong.

'He's a plain, wholesome man,' Aunt Dizzy had commented about Ivan. 'Straightforward. Obviously middle class, which is why he hasn't much to say. Boring, in fact. And he snores, when he isn't talking to himself. I should have moved downstairs, Jean, when you kindly suggested it, but there's no accounting for us women. We *are* contrary, even if I say so myself. I'll stay where I am and suffer. One day you'll take pity on me and have a stair-lift installed.'

She had invited Ivan to join her and Christopher on several outings, but he had politely declined. The usually unreliable spring weather was so mild that Ivan had taken to sitting on a wicker chair in the garden, reading. He had joined the local library – on a temporary basis, he'd explained, and read incessantly. He apparently enjoyed the company, being at Acacia

Road, but now having shared with Jean the rudiments of his Brighton days alone he had little more to say to her or anyone except to his late wife to whom he talked, in his room at night, with what Aunt Dizzy described as vigour. Yet Ivan seemed relaxed. He smiled often during dinner. Jean had taken him out for lunch twice, but he claimed to prefer homely English cuisine. Christopher cooked. Aunt Dizzy insisted on paying the food bills. Jean found Ivan one morning with the Hoover and a duster, wearing an old apron he'd discovered hanging from the back of the kitchen door. As he dusted and vacuumed he hummed tunelessly. Christopher said he didn't mind at all that Ivan was taking on the cleaning. Jean had stopped paying him anyway.

Ivan and Jean had walked along the seafront before leaving Brighton to Palace Pier, on which Ivan insisted Jean stroll with him, right to the end and back, stopping to gaze at its fairground attractions and shops. They sat in the sunshine on deckchairs, enjoyed a drink in one of the bars, all the while Ivan talking about himself and May. He left Jean sitting in Pool Valley while he hurried back to his room to pack a bag. He'd brought two large suitcases and a backpack, as well as a plastic carrier bag filled with paperback westerns, which, he explained, he'd begun to enjoy. His taste ranged from those to political thrillers and even the occasional horror novel. He read several novels at once and had begun to leave books scattered all over the house. Aunt Dizzy thought they lowered the tone.

'I don't *mind* anyone reading,' Jean overheard her telling Christopher, 'but it's a sad-arse case who lets such common stories rule his life.'

Having dismissed Ivan as a rather dreary, crusty middle-class hindrance, she continued a new course of trying to visit every London art gallery she could find, with the idea of investing.

'We could fill this house with art, Jean,' she suggested one morning over breakfast, staring with disdain at Ivan who was engrossed in a James Herbert novel with a lurid cover. 'There's no end of wall space, ducks. Got to spend my money on something and contribute. Then when we're all headed for the flophouse we can sell them one by one and live off the proceeds. Their value does accrue, so I'm told. There's profit to be had in pictures.'

Christopher had stopped going to college. He was looking for a job. He had never wished to study further once he left school. It had been his father's idea, he told Jean one night, to study for a degree and escape the clutches of his mother.

'But what will you *do*?' she asked. Christopher had merely shrugged. They were sitting in the morning-room with mugs of hot chocolate. Ivan and Aunt Dizzy had both retired to their rooms. Christopher had asked to hear Jean singing, so she'd played him selections from two CDs. He had listened with his eyes tightly closed and told her afterwards with great emotion that her voice was *rapturous.* Then he awkwardly stood to his feet and kissed her on the forehead three times. He did not suffer from body odour any longer, so his close proximity and the kiss were bearable and almost poignant, despite the rubbery touch of his lips.

His mother had recently had a letter delivered which had been printed off a computer and pushed through the letterbox. All across the top of the letter were small coloured portraits of Jesus with a snow-white beard. The portraits looked more like Santa Claus.

We are all LOUDLY praying for you three times a day now and five times on Sundays, she wrote. *Whatever you are doing with that old woman I met you with is none of my business, but at least it will be less perverted than the company you kept with my damned-to-hell brother. As I cannot truly deny that you exist, then please expect me to keep on by letter in attempts to save you from your horrendous sins, just as I once saved your father. You will never be welcome again in my house, but I remain, in Jesus Christ's name, your loving mother.*

She had enclosed various religious tracts of a more thunderous nature, which Christopher intended to keep in a box-file beneath his bed. As, he said, there would be more. He still loved his mother, he explained. There seemed no reason, to his mind, that he should stop.

'I want to ask you something,' he said, sniffing at his fingers after picking up and discarding one of Ivan's library books, a battered, creased paperback called *Slicing the Departed*.

'Go on.'

Christopher sniggered.

'It's Uncle Fergus. He wants to know whether he can come and stay sometimes. Overnight. We won't make any noise. He likes you. He likes Aunt Dizzy. He didn't want to ask you himself because he gets depressed when people say no.'

Jean was mending a pair of Ivan's woollen socks. Ivan owned twenty-seven pairs of woollen socks. Two pairs of nylon socks Jean had managed to lose.

'You mean in your room? Or would he like to take over the last guest room?'

Christopher blushed.

'He's . . . changed his mind about things. That we should be sort of married before . . . sex.'

Jean did not look up from her mending. Christopher coughed.

'You said I shouldn't be scared of that word,' he added.

'Christopher, you'd have to be *very* discreet. And no,' Jean said at his stare of consternation, 'you haven't embarrassed me. Not at all. I was thinking of Mr Fitzpatrick. Ivan. I'm really not certain how he'd take it. He's quite conventional in his way. I don't wish to upset him. I don't want it flaunted in front of him. He might not understand. I don't see why you can't go to Fergus's house.'

'Is he staying here? Like me?'

'Possibly. I don't know. I wouldn't mind. He's got no one else. And I like him, Christopher. I know he doesn't say much, but he's had a rough time recently and he *was* my father-in-law. He was living in an awful room down in Brighton. Hove.'

They fell silent. Christopher picked up the paperback novel again and started sniffing the pages. Then he put it back and overtly wiped his fingers on his shirt. Jean watched him with a gentle smile. Christopher kept rapidly lifting his heels off the floor and letting them fall. He tapped on his knees with his hands, not looking at her.

'What sort of a job are you going to look for?'

'There's one going up at the library. Just sorting returned books. It doesn't pay much.'

'Money isn't a problem, Christopher. You know that. I shan't expect you to pay rent. If we go short you could always write a begging letter to your mother.'

Christopher sniggered.

'If you do work up at the library you could bring some decent books back for Ivan. Improve his taste. He goes up there almost every day.' Jean put down her mending and gazed up at the ceiling. 'I've never known anyone who reads so *fast*.' Then she added, 'I'm sure you could get a better job than that. There's no future in libraries, not in this country. And after all your studies . . .'

'What about Uncle Fergus?'

'I've no idea if he reads. You'll have to ask him.'

Christopher looked away. His lips sagged. He seemed as if he was about to cry. 'Oh, go on then, you're obviously anxious. Fergus can come to stay one night a week. A trial run. But he's to promise, mind – no wandering about the house wearing next to nothing as you do. Understand?'

Christopher had taken to coming downstairs in his under-wear and socks.

'Uncle Fergus would *never* walk about like that! He'd wear pyjamas and a dressing-gown. He's got five dressing-gowns. They're all silk. He bought them in Singapore.'

'*Not* even in those,' Jean said. 'No, if he is to stay overnight then he will have to be discreet. Ivan goes to bed early. What say you ask Fergus to arrive late in the evening, but you both must stick to your room.'

'OK.'

'And no loud giggling. Or laughing. I heard you with Auntie last night in her room. It was gone two o'clock before you went to bed. That must stop. I'll have a word with her. I've no idea where her energy comes from. I don't want the *three* of you holding pyjama parties or midnight feasts. Heaven forbid.'

'We aren't children,' Christopher mumbled.

Uncle Fergus often joined Aunt Dizzy and Christopher on their frequent outings. Jean had begun to suspect that they allowed Christopher to drink while they were out. She had been roused several nights ago at one a.m. by the three of them in the downstairs hall, giggling loudly after Uncle Fergus dropped them off. Ivan had been standing outside his bedroom door as Jean emerged to see what the commotion was downstairs.

'I thought it might be burglars,' Ivan had stage-whispered at her. He was wielding his umbrella like a weapon, wearing a dressing-gown the like of which Jean had not seen since the 1950s. It was all thick wool and had a rolled waist-sash with pom-poms. She had apologized to him also in a whisper, and he'd smiled sadly and gone back into his room, locking the door. He rarely failed to lock his bedroom door when he was in there. She heard him talking to May.

Jean had found Christopher lying on his back on the hall carpet, kicking his legs in the air. He wasn't wearing shoes or socks. Uncle Fergus was leaning over him tickling his sides. Aunt Dizzy was clapping her hands as she looked on and began to cry out 'Whoop-whoop, whoop-whoop!' All three appeared to be drunk. Getting to his feet, Christopher had then fallen over and lay on his side in a helpless fit of giggles. Jean had herded them upstairs, after sending Fergus out the door, in an angry silence.

Anthony Hibbert telephoned. He sounded rather nervous. It was late, almost midnight.

'I've bought tickets for a new production of *Butterfly*,' he told her in a clipped voice. 'Do you fancy going?'

'I'd love to. I'm surrounded by the aged and a drunken juvenile.'

'Pardon?'

'Never mind. Look, may I meet you somewhere? I'd rather you didn't come to the house right now.'

'Is something wrong? It's all right, I don't mind if you aren't interested.'

'I am. When's the performance?'

They arranged to meet along Floral Street where he said he'd take her for a meal beforehand.

'I've a friend who owns a small restaurant,' he said.

'I'm sure you have.'

'Are you all right? You sound tetchy.'

'I'm fine, Anthony. How was Belgium?'

'Beastly. You know, I really dislike English publishers when they're abroad. I've been really looking forward to seeing you.'

'As I said, I'm old enough to be your mother. *Beastly*?'

'It worries you, doesn't it? My being a little younger.'

Jean could not think of an answer. Anthony *was* less than half her age.

'Jean?'

'I'm still here.'

'It's just an evening out. I'd like an evening out with a truly beautiful woman who doesn't talk shop.'

'Oh, all right. You've talked me into it.'

After she replaced the receiver she realized that Ivan was standing in the morning-room peering through at her. The door was wide open.

'I seem to have mislaid one of my library books,' he said. 'Can't find it anywhere.' Then he stared at her with a frown. 'I've just had a fright. There's a peculiar-looking man in the bathroom doing press-ups in his underwear. He said he was Uncle Fergus. Is he a relative?'

Jean started to laugh, then stopped and didn't reply. Briskly she helped Ivan find his book. After he'd gone slowly back up the stairs looking bemused she headed for the kitchen, rummaging in the cupboards for a half-bottle of gin she kept in a cake tin.

Anthony was already waiting for her on the corner of Floral Street when she arrived the following evening. She almost didn't recognize him. He had had his hair cropped short, wore a silver ring in the lobe of his right ear and sported designer stubble. He held her loosely by the elbow as they walked back down the street to a tiny restaurant with hanging baskets of late daffodils and with gas lights out the front. Anthony kept grinning at her every time she glanced at him. He smelt delicious, in a new grey suit.

'Am I mumsy enough for you?' she asked.

He laughed. 'You look gorgeous. Edible.'

Jean had agonized over what she should wear, as if she was about to embark on a first ever teenage date. She wore black. She had remained in her rooms for two hours before leaving. Ivan had been hovering about downstairs, obviously wishing to speak to her about something. Aunt Dizzy and Christopher had gone out earlier to visit a new gallery in Camden Town which encouraged young London landscape artists and was holding a sale. Christopher had avoided her all day. He had not appeared for breakfast. Jean had burnt six slices of toast. The coffee was too strong. Ivan's tea bag had split. Aunt Dizzy sat doing *The Times* crossword all during breakfast saying almost nothing at all. Ivan sat reading a horror novel by Christopher Fowler. He kept tut-tutting until Aunt Dizzy eventually asked him with a voice dripping with frost to be quiet. Jean suspected that Uncle Fergus had stayed the night and was still upstairs with Christopher.

The restaurant was overheated and overcrowded, filled to capacity with young people, most of whom Anthony seemed to know. Several waved and stared. Two young men threw Anthony elaborately gestured kisses and stared openly at Jean with knowing smiles.

'You've two huge fans there,' Anthony whispered as they made their way across the room.

'Spare me,' Jean whispered back. He steered her to a table on its own in a far corner. Immediately they sat down two waiters who looked no older than thirteen hurried across with a Japanese screen which they deftly opened out and arranged so that Jean and Anthony were separated from the other tables.

'The advantage of having friends who own a restaurant,' Anthony told her. 'This place is always packed. I've already ordered. A drink?'

Jean realized half-way through the meal that she had never been out with anyone so attentive. Anthony did not take his eyes off her. He behaved as if there was no one within a five-mile radius.

'I've been planning this for months, you realize,' he told her. 'As well as how to have my wicked way with you.'

'It's just an evening out, Anthony. An evening out with a truly handsome young man who doesn't talk shop.'

Anthony laughed. 'So why couldn't I come to the house?'

As they ate Jean told him about her guests and her day in Brighton with Ivan. His puzzlement at finding Uncle Fergus in the bathroom. 'I've a full house,' she said.

'Seems to me you've been lonely, Jean Barrie.' Then, after she didn't respond, he said, 'I came across someone who knows you, in Brussels. Well, a couple of my colleagues did. A Miss Truman, she calls herself. Caught a glimpse of her at one of the inevitable gatherings, on the arm of one of our rivals. Kept talking about you in a loud voice apparently. The book – your book – was mentioned. Or rather its abandonment was talked about.'

'Yes?'

'Do you know her?' Anthony was watching her carefully. Rather too carefully, Jean thought.

'She was my lodger.'

'You never mentioned that!'

Jean shrugged. 'You never mention your wife.'

He blinked but did not respond. 'I thought I'd seen her before. Catherine Truman. I think I saw her a couple of times when I was coming to the house. Up near the tube. You never said a thing about her.'

'She stole a poster from the hall,' Jean said. 'She was . . .'

Just then the two young men who'd thrown Anthony kisses appeared around the corner of the screen. They were wearing identical suits.

'Hi!' they said in unison. Anthony sighed loudly. He cast Jean an apologetic smile and introduced them. They were both called Jeremy. They gushed. One of them insisted on kissing her hand. The other kissed Anthony's hand.

'Wonderful to meet you, Jean Barrie,' they said, again in unison. They told Jean they each owned a copy of every album she had ever made.

'We saw you at the Albert Hall,' the one who had kissed her hand said. 'Wonderful. *Wonderful.*'

'And so now you can piss off,' Anthony told them, grinning. 'Sorry,' he said to Jean after they'd gone. He did not mention Catherine Truman again. Jean had fallen silent at the mention of the Royal Albert Hall and was staring down at her empty plate. 'Are you all right? They weren't supposed to do that. Jean?'

'I'm fine. The meal was delicious. Really. But I'd like to go. Have we time for a walk? I'd like some fresh air.'

'Of course. Oh Christ, we should have gone to a bar or somewhere else. You haven't enjoyed this, have you?'

Jean leant across and kissed him on the cheek.

They walked slowly along Floral Street and down Bedford Street into the Strand. It was still early. The performance began at seven thirty. Away from the restaurant, to which she suspected Anthony had taken her simply to show her off, Jean began to relax. They discussed recent novels Anthony's publisher had just released, Anthony recounting stories of authors he had met, liked or disliked; the competitive, cut-throat politics of corporate publishing that he confessed to enjoy but which to Jean sounded trite or even harsh. She wondered what she was doing here with him. They arrived back at the Opera House in a silence neither was willing to break.

Some time during the second act Anthony reached across and took her hand, drawing it into his lap, entwining his fingers with hers. He did it so naturally, without any hesitation or fuss that she did not pull away, even when she realized that he had an erection.

It was gone four o'clock in the morning when she arrived back at Acacia Road by taxi. She had warned Aunt Dizzy as well as Christopher that she might be late. One hall light was glowing as she quietly let herself in. She moved straight along the hall and into the kitchen, planning to brew a mug of herbal tea. Her lips felt bruised. Her breasts ached. She was exhausted but wide awake. There was a note sitting on the breakfast table.

Look in the hall. Christopher's writing. The house was as silent as it ever could be. She retraced her steps, switching on the other hall lights. There was nothing sitting on the table beside the door. Nothing propped up on the floor. She went to turn away but then slowly realized that there was no gap along the walls any longer. Jean blinked. The framed poster was back, as if it had never been missing. Moving closer to examine it, she noticed a small plain card attached to one corner by invisible tape and that the glass had been replaced. On the card was written, *I am so sorry. Catherine.* Jean left the card where it was and returned to the kitchen. She began to feel slightly paranoid. She sat down at the table after finding an opened bottle of gin and rapidly drank three glasses. Someone upstairs was snoring, loudly.

She was woken just after ten the following morning by loud voices downstairs, one in particular, and then laughter. Still half asleep, her muscles aching, head throbbing and a sweet odour still lingering on her skin that immediately brought Anthony's face, in close up, to mind, she pulled on a dressing-gown and staggered along the hall and down the stairs.

Christopher and Uncle Fergus stood in pyjamas in the morning-room peering along the hall towards the front door. They were holding hands. Christopher was sniggering. Just inside the front door, surrounded by a mountain of luggage and dressed completely in black and white with a huge ascot-like hat on her head with a veil, stood Freida.

As soon as she saw Jean she threw up her arms in an Ethel Merman gesture and cried out, 'The Devil's Dyke has *returned* !'

TEN

Freida was upstairs with Jean, closely examining the mural on the wall of the departed Fallen Nun's rooms. As soon as she set eyes on the painting she cried out, 'Bloody Nora, Jean, it's you!' and demanded an explanation which Jean was unable to give. 'How on earth did she manage to see you in the buff?'

'It could be anyone!' Jean snapped. 'With my face.'

'And does *anyone* have that mole just below the curve of your neck? Not a mole shaped like that. It's you!'

Jean had confessed to having put the mural out of her mind. She had been too distracted to think about it.

'This speaks volumes. The artist is obviously in love with you. Or she hates you. Look at it. I knew the Nun must have been a dyke.'

'No you didn't. Stop being reactionary. Besides, she's engaged to be married.'

Freida gave Jean a tired, world-weary look and turned her gaze back to the mural.

'It's good. In fact I'd say quite stunning. Though your breasts aren't *that* small. The empty gin bottles are a bit over the top. Well, well, well. Who would have thought. I've only been gone a short while and you have a secret portrait in the attic and rooms full of drop-outs.' Freida moved to one side of the mural, turned to face Jean and added in a low, mock-serious whisper, *'What if it ages?'*

'Don't be flippant. No, I take that back. I need you to be. I'm a little bewildered.'

'Hardly surprising. Jean, Jean, it's all very well having Doo Lally here, but the others? A teenage sexually naïve giant with mega-lips who's in love with his uncle? Your ex-father-in-law who talks to his dead wife behind a locked door?'

'I shouldn't have told you that. They both needed a place to live. To stay.'

'Just like me.'

'What?'

Freida wasn't looking at Jean. She appeared to be studying the rest of the room. There was a small fitted kitchen leading off it and a bathroom. There was a wine stain on the carpet, Jean noticed, and a lingering smell of damp.

'I can't go back to the house. Now Mandy's taken over. It's why I fled. I told you.'

Freida had been in Prague. She had, one night, packed numerous suitcases and, clutching her passport, had taken a taxi to Heathrow; got on the first available flight, which happened to be heading to the Czech Republic. She had booked into an English-speaking hotel and walked the streets, as she put it, like a common tourist. Then she'd flown to New York to stay with an elderly transsexual friend who'd been a woman but decided late in life to revert, if not in a fully physical way, to being a man, because being a woman was too difficult. He lived in the Village so Freida had felt perfectly at ease, whereas she hadn't in Prague.

'She's moved in lock, stock and sex toys with her two friends. Mandy, I mean. She has a couple of simpering little queens who adore her and who she bosses about. They only look about fourteen and spend hours in the bathroom dyeing each other's hair. Mandy arrived with a van filled with everything she possesses including her boys, as she calls them, and announced she'd come to enrich my life. They're still there. So I can't go back.'

'You want to stay here?'

Freida glanced at Jean and smiled guiltily. She remained silent but nodded.

'You know I couldn't deny you,' Jean told her. 'You could stay up here or downstairs in the room I made ready for Auntie. But you can't just let this Mandy have your house. It's your home! You'll have to ask them to leave. Do *something.*'

Freida shrugged.

'I could have the locks changed. Get them thrown out. I've been planning to sell anyway, Jean. It's too big. I get lonely. Oh, what am I saying? I'm prattling. I'm jet-lagged. I refuse to face going back there. It's too humiliating after running away. She started redecorating the bathroom two days after she moved in. Painted it *pink*. Bought frilly lace for my bedroom windows and five Steiff teddy bears to sit on the bed. She gave each of them *names*. Trips about the place like some demented robotic house-wife. Like in that old film, what was it called? Where all the women got transformed. He wrote *Rosemary's Baby.*'

Jean remained silent. Freida looked embarrassed and was on the verge of tears. Jean stepped across the room and embraced her, drawing her close. Freida grew rigid, then relaxed. They were still standing like that when Christopher walked in wearing pyjamas and a silk dressing-gown several sizes too small.

'Mr Fitzpatrick's shouting,' he said. 'In his room. At his wife.' Then he stopped and stared with widened eyes at the painting on the wall. 'Jesus,' he muttered.

'No, actually it's Jean,' Freida said, pulling away from Jean's embrace. 'Did we hear you knock?'

'Sorry,' said Christopher. He stared at the painting open-mouthed and began to wring his hands. His over-large ears turned bright crimson. They matched the colour of his lips.

'Not seen a naked lady before, huh?' Freida asked. 'You've sure missed a great deal, sunshine.'

Christopher stopped wringing his hands and sniggered.

'Where's Uncle Fergus?' Jean asked.

'Gone. Had breakfast. Three slices of toast and two of bacon. He left most of the bacon. I ate it. I've made coffee.'

A voice called up the stairs.

'Cooee! Jean? Where are you? I damn near fell over all these bloody suitcases! Can't someone move them? Are you leaving? Christ, I hope not.'

Jean hurried Freida and Christopher out into the hallway before Aunt Dizzy tried to ascend the stairs. She locked the door behind her and pocketed the key.

'I don't want you telling Auntie about the painting,' she told Christopher. 'I'm serious. You weren't supposed to see it either.'

Christopher's head was turned away. 'He's stopped shouting,' he said. 'The coffee will've gone cold.'

'*Stepford Wives*,' Jean said to Freida.

'Good morning, Mr Fitzpatrick!' Aunt Dizzy's voice trumpeted upwards. There was a muttered reply Jean did not hear.

'Am I *really*?' shouted Aunt Dizzy.

'This is a madhouse,' Freida said, taking Jean's arm.

Anthony Hibbert kept telephoning. Jean kept making excuses not to see him. During the following week flowers arrived every morning. The arrangements and choice grew larger and more expensive every day. Uncle Fergus came to stay overnight almost every night, arriving sometimes past midnight and often terribly drunk, dressed in a variety of yellow, tan and orange suits. He now wore a tinted monocle. Ivan remained for hours in the garden, accompanied by piles of library books he stacked up around him on the grass like castle turrets. Jean watched him one morning, reaching for one book, reading a little, then placing it back on to a pile to take up another. His actions became rather frenzied, as if he was searching for something within the books' pages he was desperate to find. He took out with him a flask of tea, a blanket and sandwiches as though he was under siege. Mrs Meiklejohn had begun to greet him across the dividing wall in an ingratiating voice.

Aunt Dizzy spent her time bringing paintings back to the house she had purchased and was stacking them willy-nilly along the walls of the front hall, in readiness, she explained, of their being properly sorted and hung. Most of the paintings were scenes of London that Jean believed were sold cheaply in large numbers at tourist markets. None were well rendered. Most had hideous, garish frames, but at least they were originals and not prints.

Christopher had taken the job at the library and confided in Jean that there were increasing complaints about Mr Fitzpatrick, who, being allowed to take out fifteen books at a time, was doing so every day and then returning them the next. Christopher had not confessed that Mr Fitzpatrick lived in the same house as he was too embarrassed. Everyone was laughing at him behind his back but were terribly polite to his face. The librarians were becoming irritated by his daily appearances and almost total lack of respect.

Freida, installed in the renovated front room, slept for most of the day, getting up and going out only after dark. She had gone to her house in Chiswick twice by taxi after dark and on each occasion stood opposite in darkened shop doorways and watched, as she put it, hordes of young gay and lesbian party-goers pouring in and out of her house as if it had become the latest, trendiest club.

'Some of them I even *know*,' she admitted. She had bought an overwhelming amount of expensive makeup accessories to cheer herself up and spent much of her time in her room trying out the latest products and entertaining Christopher, who she'd taken a liking to, with diet cokes and digestive biscuits. One morning Jean found Christopher in the kitchen making coffee in full makeup and wearing enormous false eyelashes. Jean was mostly left to her own devices and allowed to take on the role of housekeeper. Sometimes Aunt Dizzy came to sit with her in the morning-room late at night, where Jean sat with a gin or a wine bottle near by for comfort, listening to music and utterly exhausted.

'*She's* got young Christopher in her room again,' Aunt Dizzy would say, having made herself comfortable in the best armchair, putting plastic rollers in her wig and with a lit cigar resting in an ashtray beside her. 'She's stolen him from me, Jean. It isn't fair. She's an usurper. I know she's your best friend, but she couldn't possibly have anything more in common with the lad than I have. Uncle Fergus is not happy, I can tell you. He told me in the strictest confidence that he fears Christopher might desert him. He doesn't deserve that at his age.' Jean had been quietly consuming glass after glass of a cheap Hungarian wine at the time and would have been perfectly content to be left alone. William had failed to reappear. He had not telephoned either, from New York or anywhere else. She was uneasy about the framed poster of herself that Catherine Truman had apparently stolen and returned. Christopher had found it on the front steps and brought it indoors. When she'd taken it down from its place in the hall where he'd rehung it, to look at it more closely, she realized that it had, sometime during its absence, been removed from its frame and then rather unprofessionally put back. There were two small rips in one corner that she was certain had not been there before. Freida was too distracted by her home invasion to be sympathetically interested. Aunt Dizzy was obsessed with her almost daily outings to buy paintings and now with her conviction that Christopher was being led astray. Christopher was simply being Christopher. Ivan Fitzpatrick continued to keep speech to a minimum and to hide himself behind his mountains of library books. He had also begun to have long chats with Mrs Meiklejohn. Jean suspected that he had been to visit her. In a house full of guests Jean had no one to talk to. She felt more isolated than when she had been alone. She was growing addled and was losing patience. Anthony was poised with bated breath, it appeared, for her to call him. Every note, with the daily flowers, professed as much. Jean began to spend more and more time alone in her room upstairs. It was the largest bedroom in the house, and the solidity of the walls and the solid, extra-thick door offered certain quietude, away from the business of the others which had begun to pall. Especially when Uncle Fergus was visiting or staying overnight. He, Aunt Dizzy, Freida and Christopher suddenly began to get together in the drawing-room, on Aunt Dizzy's suggestion, to play charades. *Noisy* charades.

'You should join our happy band, ducky,' Aunt Dizzy suggested. 'We're working on Ivan the Terrible, to get him away from all those revolting books. It's like the old family gatherings. It'd do you the world of good. A few laughs a day keeps the doldrums at bay. You brood too much. You drink too much. You're alone too much. At least we still have our little late-night chats.'

Aunt Dizzy confessed to not needing much sleep. She would creep downstairs well after midnight in her floor-length chartreuse dressing-gown, just as Jean was settling in to listen to music through headphones, everybody else in their own rooms and, it was to be hoped, asleep. There was little time during the day to seek solitude. Christopher had stopped preparing break-fast every morning. Jean prepared breakfast and lunch, even dinners, and often found herself cleaning and vacuuming, as Ivan had given that up. She attended to Ivan's washing which he left outside his door, was consulted by Freida about 'new looks', she pretended to admire each new batch of amateur paintings Aunt Dizzy brought home. Now there were paintings stacked in the reception room as well as along the hall, with more upstairs. Ivan kept suggesting they invite Mrs Meiklejohn across for tea and had mentioned it now seven times. Flowers, from Anthony, kept cluttering every surface. The downstairs rooms resembled a florist shop amidst a downmarket art gallery. While up in the Green Room, the almost nightly charade parties escalated into formal gatherings where Aunt Dizzy, smoking her cigars, presided over the proceedings and entertained the troops by holding karaoke nights from which Jean hid, in her room, wearing ear-plugs she had gone out to buy from Boots the Chemist.

Such a gathering was seemingly getting out of hand late one night, when Jean heard the doorbell ringing. She had declined to go upstairs to join the others, even after being told that Ivan had finally, though reluctantly, agreed to join in. The noise was deplorable. She was sitting in the kitchen deciding whether or not to give up and join the happy band herself or go out for a walk. Aunt Dizzy had bought a hymnal and the evening's chal-lenge was to sing a hymn but change the words – the most obscene renditions would win. Jean sat in her coat, sipping vodka. The spring weather was rapidly evolving into what was being predicted as the hottest summer weather to come in London records. The evenings were so balmy they invited escape.

Anthony stood on the front steps. At least, she thought, he

had not brought flowers. Jean stared at him blankly. He was clean-shaven but without a tie. His eyes were bloodshot.

'I'm in love with you, Jean Barrie,' he said, gazing at her with alcohol-driven urgency. 'I couldn't bear it any longer, so here I is. Am.' He leant against the door-jamb dissolutely, threatening to slide to the ground.

'There's something else. I –'

'You are drunk,' Jean said, interrupting him.

'Drunk with love. With adoration. Lust.'

'Rubbish. You'd better come in. The whole damn world's upstairs. Partying.'

He followed her along towards the morning-room.

'Lovely flowers,' he said.

'Shut up.'

From upstairs laughter and shouting drifted down, growing louder all the time. Freida shouted, 'Ride it, Ivan. Ride it, man!' and Aunt Dizzy was whooping. Jean went straight through into the kitchen.

'I'll make some strong coffee,' she said. 'Sit down.' But when she turned Anthony was not behind her. Retracing her steps, she found him half-way up the stairs and grabbed his arm, pulling him back so roughly he tripped and fell and yelled out, the sound lost beneath the noise from above. He sat down heavily on the stairs with his head in his hands until suddenly, without warning, he leant forward and vomited all over his trousers and shirt and shoes. He had pulled off his jacket, which lay on the morning-room floor.

Fifteen minutes later he sat at the kitchen table in his underwear, bare-footed, sipping coffee and groaning. Jean had rinsed out his clothes and hung them to dry in front of the warmed oven on a chair. They'd been covered with half-digested food. Some of it had even seeped into his shoes.

'I've something to tell you,' he eventually mumbled, his words slurring.

'You already have.'

'No. No, not that. It's true though. I'm in . . . in . . . I love you.'

'Well, go home and take a large bottle of aspirin and a bottle of whisky. In the morning you won't have to face any more suffering.'

'Cruel. That's a really cruel thing to say.'

Jean stood with her back to him, staring out the windows. She focused on her reflection in the glass. She remembered staring at her reflection in the same glass the night William had told her he was leaving, after throwing things out into the street in a tantrum. There had been moonlight; there was no moon now. The garden was pitch black beyond the pale lemon light from the kitchen.

'I've some bad news.' Anthony was not slurring his words. She glanced round at him. He was staring at her so intently she moved and sat down opposite. His face was stricken.

'What's wrong?' she asked. 'What's happened?'

He stared at her as if considering his reply, licking his lips. He stank of vomit which she tried to ignore.

'There's a book coming out,' he said, perfectly clearly. 'Next month, in the States. Guess what it's called? Go on, guess.'

'*The Naked Ape?*'

If Christopher had been in the room, she thought, he would have sniggered. Anthony just stared.

'I'm not joking.'

Something in his expression stopped her from trying to think of a snide remark. 'Go on,' she said.

'It's called *Lady Sang the Blues*.'

'Wasn't that a film? Billie Holiday. Who was it who played her? Lovely, lovely voice. Oh Lord, I'll remember in a minute.'

Anthony remained silent for a long moment. He sipped his coffee and stared down at the table, shaking his head.

'It's about you,' he said eventually. 'You. Jean Barrie. I heard about it this morning, so I went out and got drunk. There's nothing can be done.'

'What do you mean? About me?'

'It's one of those, what's the word . . . exposures. Trash trade paperback. A new paperback house just formed in New York. Gossip. Drivel, scandal and speculation. Part of a series. You're number three. They've already done an actor and some television personality. You're the singer target. Deliberate crap. The book will sell. Millions.'

'You *are* joking.'

Anthony shook his head vehemently. Then he grinned. 'Well, thousands, then.'

Jean gave him a withering glance and asked, 'Can they do this? Just anyone, publish such a book? Without even *telling* me?'

'Not just anyone.'

Jean got up and rummaged in the cupboards for another bottle of comfort. There were three empties on the shelf. She found a half bottle of sherry and poured a glass, downing it with her back to him.

'Go on,' she said quietly.

'It's been written – hacked together – by someone you know. Someone who was once . . . close.'

'William.'

'No.'

When he didn't say anything more she banged her glass down with such force it jumped out of her hand and fell to the floor and bounced. She turned her head and gave him a baleful glare.

'Truman,' he said, not looking her in the eye. 'Catherine Truman.'

In the ensuing silence there was a scratching sound from inside the walls. Upstairs, laughter and voices continued to swell and subside like storm waves.

Jean kept her back to the room.

'Rats,' she said. 'Ruddy, stinking, bloody, fucking rats.'

ELEVEN

In the early summer heat London is languishing. Already there are dire warnings from pernicious weather predictors of water shortages to come. A multitude of skin-protection creams are being advertised on television. The River Thames has begun to smell, according to a newspaper report Aunt Dizzy reads out one morning to Jean and the others over a cold breakfast.

Uncle Fergus now keeps three canary-yellow suits and matching ties in Christopher's wardrobe. He has his own pink toothbrush with an enamel mug in the bathroom. The karaoke nights and evenings of charades in the drawing-room have ceased; replaced by occasional gatherings on the lawn once the sun has gone down. Aunt Dizzy wears hot pants during the day, left over and still fitting her from the sixties. Her legs are surprisingly devoid of varicose veins or other age-related blemishes. The house sits uneasily, beneath the rising heat of the early summer days. During the nights it has begun to complain in subtle ways. Cracks have appeared in the ceilings of the rooms of the departed Fallen Nun and also in one of the bathrooms. The floors creak loudly when no one is moving about. Christopher swears that unused electricity in the walls is again chattering and that along the upstairs hallways he has seen shadows of the long departed lingering in the dusk. Sometimes in the mornings while he soaks his body in a bathful of warm water, to which he adds several drops of bleach, he marvels that he is not a virgin any longer and that he is *deeply* in love with his uncle.

Uncle Fergus, who is at the house so often that Jean has more or less given in to letting him be there whenever he likes.

Two streets away, a woman who has lived off the dubious fame of having been the star of a popular long-running series of television advertisements for pasta has returned to her unoccupied house after a difficult breach birth. The baby has died. By late afternoon she will also be dead, from swallowing two full bottles of sleeping pills with the aid of freshly squeezed orange juice and vodka.

On the southern slopes of Primrose Hill, two men of uncertain age and nationality who have never met before have been enjoying vigorous, silent oral sex in the bushes. Now that it is first light, and they have finished, they are sitting apart on the grass, enjoying the warmth of the rising sun, casually discussing unusual websites on the Internet. It is dawn on a Friday. Most of the world near by is still asleep or at least still in its pyjamas.

Jean is sitting in her nightclothes in the morning-room, clutching a mug of freshly brewed German coffee, the beans of which Christopher bought and had ground in the high street. Jean is alone, her legs drawn up beneath her on the chair. Her face is decidedly pale. She has not brushed her hair or her teeth and has been awake for most of the night. Her thoughts vaguely run along the lines of whether she *should* have an affair with a 25-year-old who is still married but not living with his wife and what to do about the American-published book on aspects of her life. A book that is apparently tantamount to being defamatory. She has not actually seen a copy of the book, but Anthony Hibbert has read sections of it to her over the telephone. It has yet to find a publisher in London and is looking less likely to. A fact which, Anthony tells her, has surprised everyone, as it implies good taste within the corporate publishing world. The book's cover is a photographic monochrome negative reproduction of the mural upstairs.

The house is broodingly quiet. Dust motes hover in the air of the morning-room. Upstairs, Aunt Dizzy is awake and sitting patiently on the toilet with no great expectations. Christopher lies within the thin and bony, pale-fleshed arms of his beloved Uncle Fergus, who is gently snoring. Ivan Fitzpatrick is lying on his own bed reading. Caught up unexpectedly in a tense, horrific moment inside a cellar where a young woman is about to be beheaded, he ignores the fly which is circling the ceiling light, like a miniature jet waiting for permission from a control tower to land. Ivan lies on top of his blankets and sheets, naked. He has thick salt-and-pepper hair from the top of his chest, across to both his nipples and right down to his groin. He keeps tut-tutting and sighs deeply.

In the front reception room, Freida Weinreb is surfacing from dreams in which she has been pursued by an electric-blue robotic housewife without a face. She is blinking rapidly as she rises from her bed and pulls on a dressing-gown made of silk, covered with Beardsley illustrations. In bare feet she tiptoes along the hall and stands for a moment gazing through into the morning-room at Jean. Her eyes, then her heart, become filled with a kind of yearning.

Jean and Ivan were sitting in wicker chairs in the garden. Freida had gone to her hairdresser, as she usually did on a Friday morning, to have her legs and armpits waxed as well as her hair trimmed. Aunt Dizzy was out with Uncle Fergus and Christopher, being treated to a full English breakfast at a truck-drivers' cafe just beyond Golders Green. It is Fergus's treat, at a sawdust-and-fried-sausages venue that fills him with nostalgia for his long-lost youth, when meeting truck-drivers while eating fried sausages was a pastime. Aunt Dizzy has purchased an expensive new wig, a marvel, she claimed, of modern wig technology. She has worn it on the outing. Fergus was still planning to take everyone to his country seat in Cheshire, but there was a complication of whether Ivan Fitzpatrick should be invited. Ivan rarely speaks to Fergus and Christopher. He told them tersely but politely, a week before, that they were perverted. He has not spoken to them again, nor to anyone else expansively except Jean, to whom he is about to reveal his lonely grieving heart and the reasons for his excessive reading.

'May met a writer, a young novelist, many, many years ago,' he began. They were sitting surrounded by library books, mostly paperbacks with bright covers and broken spines. Jean had finally plucked up enough courage to ask him why he was reading so much. She had made coffee. It sat in a percolator alongside cups on a third wicker chair.

'She claimed she met him at the Odeon cinema in Brighton one rainy afternoon. She had begun to visit the cinema in the afternoons back then, once or twice a week, by taxi. She never told me. They began talking during the interval. She was never to tell me until years – decades – had gone by, years after the friendship that she kept secret. And then it was because she knew she was dying. I was never to discover the author's name. She refused to tell me. By that time, of course, it was all long over. The friendship dissolved when the man went abroad and never came back. They met several times, before he proposed something to her over lunch that she was to agree to.'

Ivan sat staring down at the books on the grass, then up at the whiteness of the sky. It was already hot and it was not yet even noon. There had been no rain for a week. By the end of each day the heat remained, and so the nights had also become still and airless. No one in the house was sleeping well. There were dark patches beneath Ivan's eyes. His lips looked bloodless.

'This man, whoever he was, utterly convinced May that she would make a perfect . . . puppet. I can't think of a more appropriate word. The idea was for her to act out scenes from the writer's mind so that he could then visualize them enough to write them down. I know that he was not a well-regarded author. Certainly not . . . literary. Ignored by the establishment. He wrote action – thrillers and suchlike, some horror apparently. May refused outright to reveal his identity or anything about him. She would meet him, eventually, at a house, and there she would become some character he was inventing. She would be given the character's name, clothes to wear which the alleged writer provided, and do as she was told. She confessed, Jean, that she had found it wholly satisfying. It settled something. Something within her. And, looking back, all during those months – years – we were at our happiest. I had absolutely no knowledge of what was going on at the time. I was away from the house all week, home for the weekends. I was often up here in London. May *was* lonely, deeply so. Yet I shall never understand why this . . . this *occupation* attracted her and therefore helped us.'

Mrs Meiklejohn was watching them from her upstairs bedroom window. Jean waved and smiled, but Mrs Meiklejohn quickly withdrew from sight without acknowledgement. Ivan did not seem to notice. Jean remained silent.

'Mock sex was involved, apparently, though May flatly refused to divulge details. There was mock violence, renditions of Gothic bloody horror, all carried out without, she said, the slightest threat of injury or debasement. Later on she would dress as various male characters and act out other roles. Sometimes with the writer joining in and two others who visited. It was all above board, she told me. She was paid for her time.

Treated with respect. Meanwhile novels would be appearing during those years, in which she was featured and described in variations of disguise. She never, as far as I knew, brought any of the books home. And all that time our marriage was as harmonious as ever a marriage could be. May became loving and gentle, the mood swings she had suffered from before and which had worried me deeply just dissipated. I suspected, for a long time, that she was under some sort of treatment. Drugs or what have you, but there was no evidence of that. We had separate rooms, you see, Jean, had had for many years. William had gone, left home, moved up here by then, still in his late teens. He never knew. The extraordinary thing was that May and I were *happy*. Genuinely so. And all the while she was meeting this man – this *writer* – who was, to all intents and purposes, using her to act out his fictional fantasy.'

'I've never told anyone else. I didn't really wish to tell you, but I did not wish you, of all people, to think I was, let us say, eccentric, reading all these books. Wondering. I am not, I must admit, altogether happy living here, my dear. I do not feel comfortable with your friends. Yet you have been so kind to let me stay. I don't wish to seem ungrateful. You deserved an explanation.'

'Perhaps you might like to move upstairs,' Jean said quietly, sensing that in the silence that followed Ivan expected such an offer. He was not looking at her directly. 'Once I have the rooms redecorated. Painted. They're in need of it. You would have more privacy.' She could not bring herself to mention the mural.

'Well, I don't really wish to return to Brighton.'

'Then don't.'

Ivan looked straight into her eyes.

'I fear I've become obsessed,' he said. 'I keep thinking it's because I left Brighton. When I was down there May seemed close. In a bizarre way I kept expecting to see her. Somehow that was worse.' After a pause, during which he picked up one of the library books, stared at its cover in distaste and put it back on the pile, he said, 'I'd had this rather useless idea that's become an obsession. If I hunted through enough books from the library I might somehow come across a clue, a cross-reference. A shadow of her. I don't know, something that might tell me who the writer was. Once I started I haven't been able to stop. There are so *many* of them, Jean. Novels. Writers. I occasionally get caught up in such grisly tales I feel I'm losing balance. It's a hopeless task. Pointless really. May did say that I would never discover the author's name, that I shouldn't even try. When she told me the story she was terribly weak and frail. All I could feel was jealousy, a kind of jealous rage that this man, this anonymous *writer*, had had the power to make May happier than I was ever able to. I loved my wife. I loved her deeply. I worshipped her. Now all I can think about is that it was not me who had made her happy after William left but someone else. A stranger. What kind of a husband did that make me?'

'You loved her. You took care of her. She must have loved you to have stayed with you until she died. You couldn't possibly have *guessed* what was happening.'

Mrs Meiklejohn had appeared in her garden. Jean suddenly noticed her – or the top of her head – and wondered if she had been eavesdropping. With his back to the wall, Ivan did not appear to realize she was there. Mrs Meiklejohn hovered for a moment or two, then went back indoors, slamming her door so loudly it startled them both. Ivan grinned.

'She's been making certain overtures,' he suddenly said in a stage whisper, then laughed.

'You've been over there, haven't you?'

'I confess! Yes, I have. She's undeniably lonely. Seriously

uneducated. She asked me endless questions about your other . . . guests. I was discreet.'

'It hardly matters.'

Jean told him a little about the book, *Lady Sang the Blues*. She did not mention the cover. He listened without comment, frowning, shaking his head.

'I would not be at all surprised', he commented, 'if my son wasn't involved in some way. Are you sure he wasn't?'

Jean nodded. She began to gather the coffee cups together and stood up.

'If I leave you alone,' she stage-whispered back, 'your little friend might come out again to play.'

Ivan laughed. Leaning towards her he took her hand and drew it to his lips. 'That might provide some intrigue, if she's still watching.'

Half-way up the garden Jean turned her head and looked back. Ivan was watching her.

'I am sorry, Ivan. I'm sorry you've had that to contend with, about May.'

'We all have something, my dear. Everybody's closets are full.'

Later in the afternoon he came to tell her that he would be interested in renting the upper rooms, so long as it was done officially. He could pay her from his pension. Jean agreed, promising that he could move in once she had had the walls painted. No, she thought. One wall.

'And Brighton?' she asked.

'I'll phone the landlord. Give him notice. I haven't left much behind. Almost nothing. I could fetch the rest of my things sometime. I would like to stay on, Jean. For a few months at least. If you respect that what I have told you is in the strictest confidence.'

'I shan't breathe a word. My lips are sealed.'

'Am I obsessed, do you think?'

'You're still in love with your wife,' Jean told him. 'It's as simple as that. I'm so glad you want to stay. I like having you here.'

'I'm a lost cause.'

'So am I, Ivan. So am I.'

Turning away, Jean had a sudden urge to burst into laughter but resisted.

Freida had done nothing about her home invasion. She was out a great deal during the day and treated the house as if it was a hotel. Jean did not mind. She had become so used to her aloneness before the others had moved in that she'd come to value it; she was perfectly willing to let each of her guests seek out and maintain their own equilibrium, without intrusion into her own life. Yet they were, of course, intruding.

She decided to paint over the mural upstairs herself, telling no one. She slipped out to buy the paint, applied layer after layer over several days until she was sure the mural would not show through. She tidied the rooms, cleaned the tiny kitchen and bathroom, adding touches she thought Ivan might appreciate. There was an abundance of bookshelf space. She saw no reason why he should give up his novel quest, if it helped him. She doubted that it did.

Freida was not happy with the idea of Ivan taking over the tiny apartment when Jean told her. She was furious that Jean had painted over the mural. 'Damned waste, Lady. Damned waste,' she said. Jean had just agreed, after a telephone call from Anthony, to go out with him for a meal at Swaheenee's, a new, expensively trendy restaurant in Soho. She was feeling almost ebulliant at the thought of seeing him again.

'I'm having an affair with Anthony,' she told Freida. 'Or I'm about to. I've just decided.'

'Affairs are out, Lady. You will be having a *relationship*. I could quite easily be envious. If he were a female I'd put poison in your gin. I shall pray that the hidden mural *won't* age.'

They were sipping glasses of mother's ruin, sitting – sprawled – on Jean's bed, backs propped up by cushions and pillows. It was late. There was no air, despite the windows being open.

'You knew I had my beady but gorgeous eyes set on that little attic,' Freida told her. 'You might have asked me first. You're a selfish bitch. You always were. Just because I'm rich. I could have lain in bed naked and gazed at the mural with unbridled lust.'

'Shut up and drink your gin, you dear, sweet trollop.'

'Do you want me here? I could just as easily be in a hotel.'

'Never! I'm pleased you're here. Honestly. I'd like you to stay. Sell the house! Or at least get that Mandy out somehow and rent it. You'd get a small fortune. Carefully chosen clients. A good agent.'

'Maybe. Right now I'd rather sell.'

'Squatters have rights.'

'She has keys, Lady. I asked her to move in. She'll screech. I couldn't stand all the upheaval of a battle. I'm too lazy to cope.'

'Well, you can't just leave things as they are. Pass me the bottle.'

There was a gentle knock on the door. It was one o'clock in the morning. Jean had heard Aunt Dizzy, Christopher and Uncle Fergus coming in an hour earlier, while Freida had been asleep on the bed.

'Are you a lady?' Freida called. 'Ladies only if you please!'

The door opened and Christopher put his head through the

gap. He stared at Frieda and sniggered. His lips looked bruised and larger than normal. They were the colour of bruised plums.

'Aunt Elizabeth has thrown up all over my bed,' he said matter-of-factly. 'It's soaked through to the mattress.'

'Drunken old slut,' Freida muttered. Jean went to get up, but Freida stopped her and poured more gin. 'Can't *you* take care of it, Big Ears? Jean and I are discussing serious political issues here, sunshine.'

Christopher's head withdrew.

'I must put a stop to Auntie staying out until all hours,' Jean said. 'I really don't know how she manages it. Eighty-one years old and she carries on like some glue-sniffing teenager.'

'Tough stock. It's the bloodline. And she's done nothing all her life, so let her have some more fun before the rot sets in. It can't be long.'

Jean allowed Freida to stay the night in her bed. They kissed drily, like sisters, before sleeping. Hours later Jean awoke and thought she could hear Aunt Dizzy along the hall, singing a Cole Porter melody perfectly in tune. Freida had a hand resting on Jean's right breast. Jean slapped it away.

TWELVE

Christopher is standing half-way along the first floor hall in his pyjamas, staring at two indistinct and shadowy figures gazing back at him. He does not speak. The figures do not speak. They are vaguely eighteenth century in their style of dress, two women of indeterminate age and class. After a moment they slowly dissolve and are gone. Christopher's bottom is dully aching. He has applied a salve and been downstairs for a glass of milk which he warmed first in a saucepan. Uncle Fergus, replete from sexual exertion, is fast asleep in Christopher's untidy bed. One blanket lies on the floor. The nights are too warm and they'd both lain together perspiring under the top sheet after making love. The top sheet is damp from perspiration. It is three o'clock in the morning.

Jean is lying in her bed in the arms of Anthony Hibbert, who has instigated divorce proceedings against his wife through his solicitor. He has asked Jean to marry him, but she has declined. Yet they are lovers. Jean is Anthony's beloved. Jean enjoys Anthony's considerable physical charms and his manner towards her which could be likened to a puppy with an indulgent owner. She is fond of him.

Aunt Dizzy lies asleep in her bed surrounded, on the floor, by paintings. She dreams of the 1930s when she was young enough to take flattery and compliments and flirtations for granted. She whimpers in her sleep, turns over without fully waking. Her toenails, which need cutting, scrape on the silken sheets. Figures, a little similar to the figures Christopher has just witnessed, hover in her dreaming sight and speak to her in admiring tones.

Downstairs Freida is lying back to back in her bed with a younger woman called Colette Carson, who is from California and came to London to reinvent herself. She was able to do so as she is rich and has connections and reinventing oneself in California has become too *passé* and common. Colette Carson is hoping to start a new trend, for she believes, being American, that no one else in England could possibly have thought of the idea of reinvention. She has opened an art gallery and exhibits semi-professional work she imports from gifted male friends in San Francisco. There is also a hairdressing salon in the gallery and a café. Colette has restyled Freida's hair, so Freida has allowed her to share her bed. They have also made love, at just after midnight. Colette's real name is Anna Chilenski. She is part Chinese on her mother's side. She has taken her adopted names from two female authors who are dead but still revered. In several hours' time Freida will wake Colette Carson and cheerfully send her packing, having tired of her strident accent.

Ivan Fitzpatrick has been sleeping but is now awake. He is happily ensconced in the studio apartment at the top of the house and, during the day, haunts second-hand bookshops, having exhausted the local library. The longing to discover whose puppet his late wife had been when they were young is slowly leaving him. There are not many lurid or salacious books on his shelves. Sitting there instead are copies of novels from Victorian authors Ivan has suddenly come to admire. With the little spare money he has left he buys cheap second-hand republished paperbacks and aged copies of such luminaries as E.H. Yates, Charlotte Yonge, John Strange Winter (who was really a woman), George Alfred Lawrence and Jessie Fothergill. Ivan speaks of these novelists to Jean, who has never heard of them, with reverential awe.

The house is serenely quiet now during the short, stifling summer nights. It is perhaps also asleep then. Christopher believes this is so, still standing in the upstairs hall unwilling to return to the demanding arms of his lover. There is a slight, refreshing coolness in the hallway as the night deepens towards the dawn. During the daytime – perhaps because of the sun which, this year, is unexpectedly strong and appearing more often than has been recorded for decades – the rooms of the house are certainly brighter. Hidden corners, which have habitually been dark when Jean lived alone, have brightened. The morning-room is flooded with early light; it has been thoroughly cleaned and dusted by Ivan and Christopher, who now, warily, speak to each other politely. The carpet has been professionally shampooed. Some of the armchairs sit closer to the french windows, which are left open all day, so long as at least one guest, or Jean, is at home. Jean refuses to take money from Ivan for his living upstairs; Freida and Aunt Dizzy contribute lavishly to the household expenses so that they all live well at Acacia Road.

Freida has put her house in Chiswick into the hands of her solicitor, who passed it into the hands of a manipulative estate agent. With help from sources unremarked or revealed the agent has been able to evict Mandy and her two young cohorts, because evicting them would not make them homeless. Naturally, money changed hands. Mandy owns a modest property in Putney and has moved back there, quite happily and without protest, with her organic and inorganic possessions. Freida's house lies empty but is being viewed almost daily by conventional married couples with children. It will soon be sold. Freida is content, for the time being, to remain at Acacia Road. She has been in love with Jean for years but will never admit it, even to herself.

A dead sparrow lies moistly in the gutter along the left-hand eave of the house. Its tiny feathered corpse is slowly decomposing with the help of enthusiastic maggots. It lies beneath a covering of leaf mulch, and no one knows it is there. Christopher, in the upstairs hall, still unwilling to return to his room, stands on one leg examining the sole of his left foot which is not terribly clean. A small and insignificant field mouse is standing up on its back legs down in the kitchen, sniffing the air. Startled by an imagined noise, it scuttles back under the breakfast table to a small hole in the skirting, behind which the mouse lives contentedly with its mate.

'I *know* I haven't been in touch,' Aunt Dizzy shouted into the telephone. 'I have been otherwise engaged, Ceddie. You don't have the monopoly of my valuable friendship. What? . . . *Am* I? Oh dear, well, all right, I'll have lunch with you. What . . . where? Oh, I don't know, ducks. You fix it. Come and collect. Over and out.'

She slammed down the receiver and peered along the hall to where Freida was leaning in her doorway, fanning herself with a lesbian quarterly she subscribed to.

'Honestly, Freida, I don't know why he's so upset. Cedric. Cedric Hyde. I used to call him my paramour, you know. Heaven knows why. He never married. He once said that I was the only woman he had ever adored. Well, pooh. Pooh to him.'

'You know very well he's gay,' Freida said. 'You've always known. You shouldn't neglect your old friends, Doo Lally. You never know when you might need them.'

Aunt Dizzy muttered something Freida didn't hear, then said

as she wandered off down the hall towards the morning-room, 'Gay my fanny. The bloody man's a sissy. Always was.'

Everyone at Acacia Road is a little fractious as the London heatwave grips. No one is allowed to water their gardens. There is talk of oncoming cut-off periods and brochures urging people to save, save, save. Bathe with a friend. Try not to flush the toilet more than is necessary. Purchase bottled water. Uncle Fergus and Christopher have been sharing a bath. Jean has refused to share one with Freida. She *has* bathed with Anthony Hibbert in his serviced Covent Garden apartment. She is still refusing to marry him. It is to be her fifty-eighth birthday in a few weeks and she believes, hopefully, that everyone has forgotten.

Christopher's mother has continued to send him letters of contrition and accusation. *I am so ashamed of you,* she writes in her letters. *I am also thoroughly ashamed of your father, who defends you constantly.* Accompanying her urgings for Christopher to seek forgiveness in Jesus Christ, she encloses religious tracts by the handful, often ones she has sent before, as there is not an endless choice. BE SURE YOUR SINS WILL FIND YOU OUT! blazes one brochure's heading. BEING QUEER IS THE PATHWAY TO HELL was another, which Christopher showed Freida to ask if it was illegal to have such things printed. Freida had laughed but was privately shocked. *I will not give up my quest to save your soul which is in jeopardy, son,* Mrs Harcourt wrote in her ninth letter, pushed through the letterbox.

Jean had decided not to take legal action over the publication of *Lady Sang the Blues.* She had been to an experienced, American solicitor ('I am a lawyer,' he'd kept correcting her) in Kensington and discussed the matter with him in depth. He was an acquaintance of Anthony's, who had gone with her. The solicitor had cheerfully urged Jean to sue, as parts of the salaciously written book were little more than spurious speculation or gossip and he sensed money. It was quite apparent from the content of the book that Catherine Truman had managed to eavesdrop, secretly go through Jean's private papers, spy on her (when Anthony was visiting) and even totted up how many empty bottles of gin and vodka Jean had got through over a long period of time. The book *was* badly written and filled with typographic errors, with little form or structure. It had at least been withdrawn from sale after Jean agreed for a letter to be sent threatening legal action. As far as Jean was concerned, that was all she wished to do. Copies had appeared in one or two of the larger London bookshops but then, just as suddenly, disappeared. There was a rumour that the publisher was to close down and was to announce bankruptcy. There were brief mentions in the press, mostly in support of the book not being stocked anywhere, but reports were few and far between. Jean Barrie was big news no longer. For a while sales of her CDs did leap; royalties and payments arrived, passed on to Jean's ex-agent. The record companies involved had appeared to have lost her address. Jean refused to be interviewed by anyone. There were several requests.

'It's over,' she told Anthony over dinner. 'That part of my life is finished. Ended. That's all.'

It was reported that Catherine Truman had remained in New York. She had not married. The English press had treated her with a surprising, open contempt. She had stated that she would sue. Nothing happened. Jean ceremoniously buried the one copy of the book she had in the garden. Anthony found copies on sale – only a handful – in Oxford Street and, after buying them, ripped them up outside the shop. Jean told him he was being childish. Anthony, in return, told her that he loved her and would do anything for her.

'I'd fly to the moon and stand on a mountain to shout out your name,' he told her one particularly hot night.

'The heat's addled your brain,' Jean retorted. 'Come over here and I'll do something about it.'

She had become suddenly, wildly sexual with Anthony Hibbert. She had astonished herself, if not him. He spent almost every evening with her, either at the house or at his own apartment, which she disliked.

Christopher was sitting in the garden with Uncle Fergus when his beloved brought up the subject of their relationship. His voice drifted across the dividing wall to the ears of Mrs Meiklejohn, who, kneeling on a cushion, was weeding a small circular garden of petunias, love-in-a-mist and pansies.

'We need, my dear sweet lad,' Uncle Fergus pontificated, 'to confirm our commitment, to seek approval of our joined souls. I am thinking on it. I have spoken openly to Elizabeth, finding courage to do so. She is in perfect agreement, as I hope you are, my precious heart's desire, that we should be joined together somehow. Although, you understand, such a thing would go unrecognized by law.'

Christopher was examining the inward-turned, rather unattractive big toe of his right foot, which, as he went barefoot, he had painfully stubbed against a leg of the breakfast table while brewing tea. He sniggered, looked up from his toe and said, 'Freida said there's a priest. Ex. He does ceremonies of blessing. Private ones. He wears all the right gear, she said.'

'Aha! Then there you are, you see. You are desirous! Well, the summer will be long and gloriously hot. We can, if you so wish, make arrangements. A private blessing of our union, my heart's desire. Splendid. It would be splendiferous. We could then all disperse to the country house for afters. I can see it all now, Master Christopher. Our love blessed, sealed and celebrated.'

He leant across and, just after Mrs Meiklejohn, unseen, had struggled to her feet and was surreptitiously peering through the gap in the wall, Fergus took hold of Christopher's large-knuckled hands and drew them up to his lips. Kissing each finger with tiny sucking noises emanating from his thin lips, Christopher angling himself so that he was nibbling delightedly on his uncle's ears, Mrs Meiklejohn stared in utmost disbelief before rapidly withdrawing. Leaving her cushion where it lay, she hurried off indoors, slamming her kitchen door so loudly that a pair of collared doves three roofs away rose up into the white heat of the sky and flew towards Primrose Hill.

The two were still exercising their mutual adoration when Aunt Dizzy, dressed as usual in hot pants the colour of fresh blood and a bright yellow silk blouse, came through the open french windows arm in arm with Freida. Jean was out. With Ivan she had driven down to Brighton for the day to collect the rest of his possessions and to pay off his landlord. The landlord had bitterly claimed that Ivan owed several weeks' rent. Aunt Dizzy had been out for lunch with Ceddie, having taken Freida along at the last moment. They had drunk numerous bottles of wine and consumed large quantities of liver pâté made on the premises with crackers and home-made cottage cheese.

'You two!' she called, gesturing down the garden as she walked a little unsteadily towards them. 'We need to discuss Jean's birthday romp!'

Fergus and Christopher quickly drew apart. Mrs Meiklejohn, having rushed upstairs, was peering at them with her reptilian eye, still unseen, from behind her newly hung net curtains that she had purchased at a Selfridges sale. She had the window open and was straining to hear what was being said.

'I want Jean to have the perfect birthday surprise,' Aunt Dizzy continued. 'I need injections of ideas. I have one. Unhand each other and put your thinking hats on.'

She sat down heavily on one of the wicker chairs. There were now six wicker chairs in the garden and a small cast-iron table Freida had brought from the patio of her house. Once settled, Freida having helped, Aunt Dizzy sat with hands resting on her plump, perfectly white knees. Leaning forward she suggested her own idea to hold a garden party that would begin late in the day and carry on into the slightly cooler evening with lanterns and fireworks and games of charades and a wide array of food.

'Fried chicken wings,' Christopher said, his ears, through embarrassment, having turned the same colour as Aunt Dizzy's hot pants. 'Fried squid. Iced tea. Poppadoms with curry. Asparagus. Nuts. I'll brew the tea.'

Aunt Dizzy glanced at him as if she was concerned for his mental health. 'Excellent,' she said. 'Excellent.'

'We could dance,' Uncle Fergus suggested and then whinnied. 'In moonlight.' Then he paused and broke into song. 'By the light, of the silvery moon, I want to swoon, with my honey I'll . . .' his voice trailed off as he met Freida's gaze. She was suppressing an urge to laugh which twisted her face into what Fergus translated as a sneer.

'He has always suffered the curse of threatened insanity,' Aunt Dizzy said, patting Freida on the back as she pretended to cough. 'His entire family are quietly insane.'

Uncle Fergus again whinnied. Christopher sniggered.

'Now,' Aunt Dizzy said, 'are we sitting comfortably? Then we shall begin.'

There was an immediate silence. Mrs Meiklejohn had disappeared from behind her net curtains. Two cats, several gardens away, began to yowl at each other in mutual hatred. Christopher examined his right foot, holding it with both hands. Unseen and unheard, Mrs Meiklejohn was dialling a local number on her gold-plated, pseudo-antique telephone, standing in her down-stairs hall fighting a giddy spell brought on by a combination of excitement and revulsion.

'Is that you, Nellie?' she asked, when the dialled number was answered.

Aunt Dizzy had locked herself in her bedroom with Christopher when the doorbell rang in several short bursts. The two of them were pouring over a list of items and ideas for Jean's forthcom-ing birthday bash, as Aunt Dizzy was now referring to it. It had gone seven o'clock. Jean had only just arrived back from Brighton with Ivan's assorted treasures, which they'd carried indoors from the car. There was a huge amount in assorted boxes. Ivan collected early twentieth-century wind-up tin toys, nineteenth-century golfing equipment, owned no less than five wind-up portable gramophones – two miniature – with dozens of seventy-eight recordings. There were copies of *National Geographic* in boxes that went back to the beginning of time. Or at least Jean thought so. Everything had been stored in another room to the one Ivan had lived in on Farm Road in Brighton. He had decided, not having told Jean until they'd reached Brighton, that he could not part with anything, as he'd bought every single item with May. He and Jean had just finished carry-ing the multitude of fusty-smelling memories down the hall to the morning-room when the doorbell sounded. Jean, out of breath, decidedly grubby, hair in complete disarray and irritable beyond measure, opened the front door to a distinguished-looking gentleman in a three-piece suit carrying two ancient leather suitcases, a walking-stick over his arm.

'Yes?' Jean asked.

'So sorry to disturb you,' the figure said, staring at Jean so intently her heart began to race. 'Is Christopher here? I'm his father.'

Mr Harcourt had the same unfortunate over-large ears and a broad smile which, as he stood there, did not quite reach his eyes.

'Mr Harcourt! Is something wrong?' Jean asked. 'I'll fetch Christopher. *Do* come in.' She thought he looked rather too pale and flustered. As he put down the suitcases, the walking-stick slipping from his arm and clattering on to the ground, she noticed that his hands were trembling. He looked *ill*.

'I shan't, if you don't mind,' he said. 'Though I am feeling a mite queer. The heat perhaps . . . May I just . . .' but before he was able to finish he crumpled – collapsing, it seemed to Jean afterwards when she thought about it, almost in slow motion – to the ground. He sat on the steps like a tall, well-dressed stick insect, blinking rapidly, legs splayed out in front of him in an ungainly posture. His face was the colour of clotted cream. Jean rushed forward and grabbed one of his arms. Just as she did so she heard Christopher running down the hall and his voice, behind her, calling 'Father? *Father!*' Christopher roughly pushed past her when he reached them, knelt down at his father's side and, taking one of his hands, rubbed it frantically between his own.

'I'm all right, son, I'm all right. Or I shall be in a minute. Let me just catch my breath.'

'What is it? Is it Mother? Where *is* she?'

Mr Harcourt stared about him as if he had suddenly forgotten where he was. He continued to blink rapidly.

'She's at home, son. Nellie's all right. Nothing to fear. We've had a little set to.' Slowly Christopher helped Mr Harcourt to his feet. Jean backed away a few steps and bumped into Aunt Dizzy, who was trying to peer around her from the hall.

'She's thrown you out,' Christopher said, staring down at the luggage. '*She's thrown you out!*'

Mr Harcourt stood shaking, balanced by Christopher's grip on his arms.

'I was off to find an hotel, son. Came over a bit queer. Didn't wish to depart without a goodbye.'

Christopher turned his head and stared at Jean, his face also ashen and creased with a frown. He was close to tears.

'Bring him in,' Jean told him. 'Leave the luggage. I'll get it. Take him along to the kitchen. Put the kettle on, Christopher.'

After they moved off, Aunt Dizzy went to help Jean as she picked up the two suitcases and the walking-stick. Jean shook her head and made an exasperated sound. The evening was still too warm and the air from the street smelt sour. It was difficult to breathe. Aunt Dizzy followed as Jean began to make her way with the luggage down the hall. Freida, who had been asleep in her room, had, in the mean time, emerged and was leaning in her doorway staring, wearing the largest hair curlers Jean had ever seen. Jean ignored her and pushed past.

'What's up, Lady?' Freida called after her. 'You look as if you've been down the salt mines, girlie!'

'Oh, shut up!' Jean tried to shout, but the words came out as a squeak. Then she came to a stop, took several deep breaths and before moving on, head drawn back, she shouted, her voice rising an octave with every word, 'THE BARRIE HOTEL IS NOW FULL! ELIZABETH, GO UPSTAIRS AND MAKE UP THE BED IN THE EMPTY GUEST ROOM. FREIDA, I NEED A DOUBLE GIN. *IMMEDIATELY!*'

Freida and Aunt Dizzy rushed to comply.

THIRTEEN

'Talk about the concert,' Anthony had said, before switching on his minicorder. 'Or, rather, the Albert Hall concerts.'

Jean had almost come to the conclusion back then, when he visited the house with only a professional interest in her, that she didn't like him. He was not sycophantic, which she approved of. He was not condescending. She had found herself staring at his lips and his hands, which were perfectly shaped as well as sensual. They'd spent hours alone together by that time.

'I was asked to sing there,' she said and shrugged.

'Go on.'

The minicorder is switched on. There is a long silence before Jean speaks.

It just happened. Oh, it took a long while to organize, I expect, and I had nothing to do with that. My agent grovelled. To me. To everyone who'd listen. I'd agreed to appear. That was enough for me. There was huge pre-publicity, posters everywhere you looked. Listings magazines gave heavy coverage before and after the first night. There were to be three concerts. Each one was booked solid within days of tickets going on sale. I was asked to do one more evening, but I refused. I'd only wanted to do one. I was drinking heavily, tempted by happy pills someone was offering. Never took them. I was exhausted from travelling, flying to New York, San Francisco. Other places. William was never home. The children had almost stopped talking to me. They spent all their time, when I was here, with my mother and father.

They were living here then, of course. Quite happily. Had sold the Brighton house. William was edgy, even cold. Distant. I knew I was slowly breaking down the family from too many outside commitments, yet there seemed nothing I could do about it and I didn't think about it very often.

There is a pause. Jean coughs. Ice tinkles in a glass. She coughs again.

Rehearsals went reasonably well. I was to wear several different outfits, all terribly glam. I was fussed over and pampered. I kept forgetting the stage directions at first. I got drunk, twice. It was all done, the show, with dramatic lighting and backdrops. A fright of timing. I simply did as I was told during rehearsals and sang. Or didn't. My parents decided that they would bring the children – though they were hardly children by then – to the third, final performance. I was too caught up in myself to take much notice. The weeks that led up to the first night are rather blurred. I remember being awake at night, drinking, fraught with panic, agonizing over nagging phone calls from William. He was, I suppose, despairing of me, even then letting go. Sunday gatherings had long stopped. I was away so much that Jared and Gemma treated me sometimes like a stranger. Mother brooded, when she wasn't lecturing me about parental responsibility.

The telephone is heard. The tape is switched off, then back on.

Sorry. Freida. Where was I?

Talk about the first night.

Well, you know who was there. Just as well I hadn't known beforehand. I've never had any desire to meet any of the royal family, even minor members, but I had to. My voice was fine. I had rested. I even remembered the stage directions, tried my best not to bump into anything or trip over. There were so many – far too many – encores. Do they call them that now? Call-backs? I don't know. I sang perfectly in tune. I think. Jean laughs.

There was a party afterwards. After the first night. Interviews. Television. It all got thoroughly out of hand, as if I'd only just been discovered. I'd been singing for years. By the second night I was regretting all of it. But it went ahead, despite how I felt. Look, I don't know what else to say.

The minicorder is switched off.

'"The most dazzling performance of style and succinct originality ever seen at the Royal Albert Hall," it said in the *Observer*,' Anthony said quietly, staring at her, leaning forward in his chair. He kept glancing at the vodka bottle beside her, which was almost empty. The ice had all gone. 'All the reviews were unanimous. "Lady Jean is conquering London," someone even wrote.'

'Yes, yes. I know. Sickening, wasn't it?'

'And offers pouring in. A new production of *Sunset Boulevard* with you in the lead.'

Jean laughed, too loudly, and swallowed the last of the vodka. She stared at the empty bottle, then carefully, too carefully, placed it under her chair and pushed it away with her feet.

'Oh yes. All that. I can't talk about that.'

'Humility isn't needed here, Jean.'

'No? Tosh, tosh.'

The minicorder is switched back on.

It was all grand, grand fun and I loved every minute. Every second. Is this what you want to hear? I was – what is it? – in seventh heaven. On a roll. At the top. The world was my oyster. The whole of London worshipping at my feet. Tributes. Offers. My agent began to smile and laugh and pretend he was human. Wonderful, wonderful. Everyone was there for the final night. Except William. My father kissed me, he was so, so . . .

Jean stops. There is a long silence and she begins to weep. The sound of her weeping grows louder and more desperate. A glass crashes and Jean cries out, angrily, *Rats, bloody stinking rotten rats!*

The tape is switched off.

'I'm sorry,' Anthony said. 'I am sorry.' They had moved into the kitchen and sat opposite one another at the breakfast table. Jean shrugged. An hour had passed. She had calmed down enough to make them some tea.

'Not a lot I could do about it. This whole idea stinks. It wasn't your fault. I do my best not to think about what happened, after. There's always a reaction. If I allow myself . . . it was all a last-minute thing, my idea to drive down to Wales. I just made up my mind and no one had any choice.'

'Do you want me to record this?'

Jean shook her head.

'No! Oh maybe. I don't know. Don't interrupt. I was on such a high that night, yet I was utterly, utterly exhausted. I was over the limit. Drunk. I shouldn't have been driving. I wanted simply to be alone with Mother and Father and the children, some-where a long way from London. I wanted William, but he wasn't here. Just a few days, I told him on the phone. No need for us to wait and for him to fly back. He'd been in Singapore, you see. Too far. And I was angry at him. For not being here.'

The minicorder is switched on. Jean is not aware of it.

So, after the last night I made them all get into the car and we drove. It was terribly late. All those miles. Hours. Down to Wales, to the cottage, in the dark. We were all excited. I'd just accepted several new offers. And the Boulevard *thing had made us all laugh. Mother thought it a joke. Me? Norma Desmond? Ha! A ludicrous idea. We stopped on the way, some motorway café. Full of truck drivers. We all ate breakfast. Grilled sausages. Even Mother seemed caught up in it all despite her complaining every five minutes about the idiocy of my juvenile impulsiveness, as she called it. Wait until the morning, she said, over and over. Drive down tomorrow. The cottage is in need of repairs. We could stay in a hotel. On and on she went. I wouldn't listen. I ignored her.'*

Jean pauses.

Is that thing switched on? Turn it off. NOW, Anthony. You conned me. I'm drunk. You prick. Turn it . . .

The minicorder is switched off.

'I've nothing more to say. You can go. You tricked me. Bastard. You got me drunk on purpose.'

'Hardly! It's your vodka.'

'GET OUT! Go on, just bugger off. Leave. It's late. And don't you EVER do that again!'

'What?'

'Get me talking about Wales. I won't. I won't. Prick. Fuck off.'

'All right! Steady on. I'll go. I'm sorry.'

She walked him to the front door. It was gone one o'clock in the morning. It was freezing in the hall. He tried to kiss her on the cheek, but she pushed him away with a sigh and shuddered as she closed and bolted the door behind him. For the rest of the night she wandered the downstairs rooms of the house, drinking, muttering to herself, sometimes weeping. She was quite unaware that Catherine Truman was sitting quietly in the darkness, half-way down the stairs, having descended earlier to watch and to listen with intent.

FOURTEEN

Ivan Fitzpatrick is having a terse, whispered talk to his late wife. Sitting on his bed in his underwear and socks, he has not been able to sleep. He has made himself a mug of hot chocolate in his tiny kitchen and sits sipping it, listening every so often, as if he is waiting for May to reply. She doesn't, of course, but her voice is so implanted in his memory that he is able to speak to her and listen for replies, nodding his head or shaking it where appropriate when they come. It has rained briefly during the night and the sound woke him. It is four o'clock in the morning. The house below him seems too quiet, as if everyone has tiptoed out the front door and deliberately left Ivan alone.

Everyone else is asleep, even Mr Harcourt – Percival – in the room on the other side of Aunt Dizzy. The room had once, long ago, been a children's nursery. Mr Harcourt, who prefers that name to Percival or Percy, which he has always detested, sleeps soundly and is not snoring. His eyeballs, however, are moving rapidly from side to side, for he is dreaming of his own long-gone childhood in India. It is the first uninterrupted night's sleep he has enjoyed for many weeks. Since, in fact, his wife packed up Christopher's belongings and threw their son out on to the street in an act that had nothing to do with the Christianity she is possessed by but more to do with petulance and spite, in Mr Harcourt's opinion. Every evening and almost every night from that time Mr Harcourt had not been allowed to rest easily for hearing, plainly and with gathering momentum, Nellie

Harcourt conducting vigorous prayer meetings in the living-room of their Eamont Street apartment with members of her church. Praying, sometimes in tongues, for the soul of their wayward, sinful, shameful son and for the damnation of her evil brother Fergus.

The walls of the house are very dry. The brief rain shower merely covered the roof tiles in a thin film of damp that will evaporate as soon as the sun is up. Damp rot in the foundations has dried up or disappeared or whatever damp rot does when it doesn't any longer exist. There are still ceiling-to-floor stains of past damp, filigreed down the walls of Ivan's rooms, but they are barely noticeable. The mural of Jean below its layers of fresh paint is totally invisible. Christopher believes the house is, figuratively, being reborn.

The field mouse which has been living behind the skirting board beneath the breakfast table downstairs in the kitchen is dead. Christopher set a trap and earlier, though there was no one present to hear it, there was a sudden, muted thud and a brief squeak. The field mouse lies in the trap with its tiny back broken. Behind the skirting its mate has given birth to eight babies. Naked and pink and blind, they crawl about in a nest of shredded newspaper and Shredded Wheat which their lone parent is feeding on, the late male having dragged pieces through the tiny entrance to their home several nights before. Aunt Dizzy enjoys Shredded Wheat as a breakfast cereal and has dropped many on the neglected kitchen floor tiles which are now rarely swept.

Three houses away, along Acacia Road, an unmarried, post-middle-aged couple who have just won several thousand pounds in the National Lottery are making love. The woman is sitting astride her lover, pinching his nipples as she reaches orgasm. Her voluptuous lower thighs bounce and shiver on each side of his ample, distended stomach, which is full of spaghetti bolognese. She is crying out so loudly that it wakes the elderly gentleman next door, a retired country GP, who lies in his bed listening. The sounds from the woman fill him with nostalgia, in his half-dreaming state, for they remind him of the sounds foxes made, at night, when he lived far away in North Yorkshire.

Otherwise the street is peaceful and serene and mostly asleep at four thirty on a Wednesday morning. The unusual heatwave still holds sway. Bath water has begun to be commonly used in an attempt to save gardens and window boxes and pots of geraniums.

Jean had taken Mr Harcourt an early cup of tea and three plain biscuits. He pulled the blankets up around his chin at first, after she knocked quietly and entered his room. His two suitcases sit neatly in one corner of the room beside a wardrobe, one of them opened. On the door of the wardrobe are hanging two grey suits, one of which has a faded pink carnation in its jacket buttonhole.

'Did you sleep well?' Jean asked him. Mr Harcourt reached across and pulled his teeth out from a glass of water and, after inserting them with his head turned away, smiled languidly at her and nodded. He was wearing red-and-white striped pyjamas.

'Thank you, I did. I feel most refreshed.'

'I was going to ask Christopher to bring this up, but *he's* still fast asleep, I think,' Jean said in a whisper. She placed the cup and saucer on the bedside table and as quietly left the room, pulling the door closed behind her. It was just after seven o'clock. The summer heat was already rising. Some of Mr Harcourt's tea had spilt into the saucer.

Jean had suggested to Christopher that Uncle Fergus not stay overnight in the house while his father was sleeping in the old nursery.

'He won't mind,' Christopher said. 'He wants me to be *happy*. He said. He's had years of gross unhappiness with Mother. He's very broad-minded.'

Christopher and his father had talked in Christopher's room for a whole hour before they'd gone to bed. Uncle Fergus had stayed away but telephoned three times before midnight and once after.

'Nevertheless,' Jean went on. 'Just out of respect for your father. I never said that Fergus could be here every night, now, did I?'

Christopher simply shrugged and didn't reply. Then he grinned, his mouth, as usual when it opened, looking like it was at least a yard wide. His ears grew pink.

'We've got plans.'

'You and your father?'

'No.'

'Then what?'

'Wouldn't you like to know.'

'Don't play games, dear. You're too old. It isn't beguiling.'

Christopher sniggered. He wrung his hands and continued to grin even after Jean left the room.

Christopher had secretly confessed to Aunt Dizzy and Freida that it was to be his eighteenth birthday the same week as Jean's fifty-eighth. He had never told Jean when his birthday was and she had never thought to ask as, until he had moved into Acacia Road, he knew she had treated him merely as being part of the furniture. On his last birthday, Christopher said, he'd prepared himself a real slap-up breakfast on Jean's electric oven.

'Fresh fried squid. Large juicy mushrooms. Chips. I ate it all before she came downstairs and gave her cereal and fruit. I brewed good coffee.'

It had been Freida who had come up with the idea for a double celebration, centred on a formal blessing by her friend the ex-priest, of Uncle Fergus's and Christopher's *relationship*. Aunt Dizzy had clapped her hands at the idea. It had grown and blossomed since then, Uncle Fergus of course being let in on the secret plans and now thoroughly delighted and in approval. Christopher had not yet mentioned the event, which was to be held in two weeks time, to his father. Freida and Aunt Dizzy were to be bridesmaid and matron-of-honour, but Freida wished to reverse the roles, which would give an interesting bent. The ex-priest, whose name was Father O'Connell but who was known locally in Brixton where he lived as Fred the Frock, had been approached and was in happy agreement to undertake the blessing in the garden at Acacia Road, after which he was also happy to accept an invitation to join the garden party that was to follow. Uncle Fergus had suggested a barbecue. He would provide the necessities for that as well as fireworks. Aunt Dizzy was to organize games. Freida was to invite a select few of her more colourful but respectable friends to bolster the numbers. Ivan had not been informed but would, of course, be included. He had now taken a paternal interest in Christopher and talked to him at some length on the history of golf, to which Christopher listened artfully and with not altogether feigned interest, therefore winning Ivan Fitzpatrick over. Ivan and Uncle Fergus greeted each other civilly, but that was as far as their friendship went, as they were grown men. Aunt Dizzy was working on that, spending time with each and praising each to the other in such glowing terms as to make her out to be an intermediary of saint-like qualities.

They had managed to decide on the details of the bash rather easily, as Jean was spending more and more of her time away from the house with Anthony Hibbert. The two had been to the theatre numerous times and spent an entire day at Richmond and Kew Gardens. Jean slept at his apartment. The expected, explosive scandal of Jean's salacious biography had not eventuated. The book had simply but mysteriously disappeared from sale, just as Catherine Truman herself had apparently vanished, the entire affair being little more, as Aunt Dizzy put it, than a storm in a paper thimble. Anthony Hibbert kept two copies of *Lady Sang the Blues* in a wall safe at his publishers, wrapped in plain brown paper and tied with string. The New York publisher involved had dissolved its partnership and closed down, Anthony had been able to discover and happily inform Jean, who was suitably underwhelmed. She was adept at dismissing such matters from her mind.

'You may come *after* the blessing,' Aunt Dizzy shouted into the telephone, standing in the downstairs hall, holding two tea towels wrapped around ice cubes to her forehead. 'The blessing has nothing to do with you, Ceddie. You don't know Christopher or Fergus. What? Speak up, you dolt. Don't mumble. You'll have to do something about those loose teeth.'

Aunt Dizzy had a thumping head and was feeling every frailty of her eighty-one years. She had been out to a late-night jazz club with Fergus and Christopher two nights in succession, which had resulted in an inability to sleep the night just gone, when Jean had wanted the house quiet because of its being Mr Harcourt's first as an unexpected guest.

'Oh, I know *that*,' Aunt Dizzy was saying. 'I've always known, Ceddie. I used the word paramour lightly, didn't you realize? It was irony. I'd never have married you, ducky. You're too much of a sissy. What? *Am* I? You're such a flatterer. Well, all right, you *may* come to the blessing. You do have things in common with the grooms, I do realize that. Have you a white suit? We are all planning to wear white, like virgins. Now don't call me again today or I'll bloody change my mind. I shall lie down and behave like the delicate soul you think I am. No, no, you're quite right. I realize I do have to slow down, Ceddie . . . Yes, I *am* eighty-two later this year. You do make me cross, reminding me.'

Mr Harcourt was standing in a grey suit and a grey tie in the hall when she replaced the receiver.

'Well, good morning!' Aunt Dizzy said too loudly and winced, whereupon most of the ice cubes slipped out from the folded tea towels and fell to the floor, slithering across the worn carpet.

'Oh, leave them. They'll melt,' she added, when Mr Harcourt stooped down to try to pick some up. 'The kitchen's back that way. Christopher's there, preparing breakfast, I think. Your son. If you'll excuse me, this aged old frump is planning to spend the entire morning in bed suffering from exhaustion.'

Before Mr Harcourt was able to reply Aunt Dizzy had swept past him, still scattering the odd ice cube, disappearing into the morning-room and heading for the stairs. Christopher, who had overheard, came out from the kitchen. He stood peering along the hall at his father, wringing his hands, his face flushed.

'I've made breakfast,' he said and grinned sheepishly. 'Toast. Bacon and fried eggs. Free range. There's two sausages. I've brewed tea.'

Jean had promised Anthony that she would meet him for a quick breakfast in Soho, at a different restaurant to the one he had taken her to before but another owned by friends. She had not wished to go and therefore not be downstairs for Christopher's father when he descended. Anthony had insisted.

'I've grave news,' he told her over the telephone when he'd

called at six thirty. Jean had been awake and downstairs in the kitchen, secretly sipping a mug of gin.

'Shit,' Jean responded. 'Not more.'

He'd refused to tell her unless she met him. He was about to fly to Zurich on publishing business. 'Some damn author's broken his contract,' he said. 'They're a real pain in the proverbial, all of them. Authors. We'll be thousands down the drain if I don't go. Why me? All the man will do is talk about himself and complain.'

Jean spent twenty minutes gathering her face together by artificial means and telephoned a minicab which miraculously arrived. The restaurant in Soho was empty. One of the waiters sat with his feet in trainers up on a bare table but disappeared as soon as Anthony ushered Jean inside. Anthony had been waiting for her on the street, his face anxious, on the pavement beside him an overnight bag. He was dressed so immaculately she felt as if she were his grandmother. He kissed her fully on the lips and as he did so he squeezed her right breast and she winced but managed a smile.

'I've to be out at Heathrow in two hours,' he told her. 'Sorry. I did need to see you before I left.'

They were served herb-laden scrambled eggs and coffee. The restaurant was closed, but the meal took as long to appear as if it were open.

'Christopher's father has moved in,' Jean told him as she sniffed at the eggs and jabbed at them with a fork. 'I shouldn't be here. He'll think it terribly rude.'

'How many is that now?'

'Five. No, six. Fergus is there most of the time.'

'Why?'

'Well, because of Christopher.'

'No, I mean why are you letting them all *live* there?'

Jean poured more coffee and didn't immediately answer. She shrugged. She'd taken one bite of the eggs and pushed her plate away.

'I have absolutely no idea,' she said. 'I'm a soft touch? Christopher's father shouldn't be there for long. What is it you so desperately needed to tell me?'

Anthony stared at her, the grin on his face fading.

'It's about Catherine Truman.'

'I'm not sure I wish to know, Anthony. Unless she died.'

'She's been in a car crash somewhere in upstate New York. She's broken several bones of one leg and fractured her pelvis.'

'You brought me all the way down here merely to tell me *that*?'

'It's rather serious. She's also in a coma.'

Jean stood up, grabbing her coat. 'I couldn't care less. I have more sympathy for the tiny mouse Christopher caught in a trap. I am going home. Honestly, Anthony, this is ludicrous. You could have easily told me – *if you had to* – over the phone. I've enough to think about right now without . . .'

'I love you, Jean Barrie. I really want you to marry me.'

Jean paused in the act of pulling on her coat, sudden anger suspended. Anthony stood up and, arms at his sides, was staring down at the table like a lost child. His voice sounded almost desperate.

'That isn't news either. I know you love me. You don't stop telling me. You're not even divorced yet.'

'It's true.'

'What on earth am I going to do with you? Really.'

'Marry me.'

'Go to Zurich. Sort that out first. Then we'll talk.'

'Promise?'

Jean nodded. They stood gazing at one another in silence until Anthony said, his voice just above a whisper, 'I'll pester you until you give in, you know. I want to share my life with you.'

'Is it true, about Catherine Truman?'

'Yes of course! We heard last night, by fax from the New York office. We've still a vested interest in you.'

Jean's anger returned. She felt like hitting him with a clenched fist.

'And is *that* why you wish to marry me? So you can pester me about my past whenever you wish? You're still planning to publish? I'm your path to riches? Ha! Prick!'

'No! That's not true.'

Anthony moved across to her around the table and took hold of her hands.

'I'll call you tonight, from Zurich. It'll be late. Please?'

Outside he hailed a black cab and was still standing with his bag, watching her, as the cab slowly manoeuvred down Brewer Street and turned right. She watched him through the rear window until he was out of sight, just standing there, smiling slightly, and she realized that her heart was thudding and that her mouth had gone quite dry and it was just possible that she might love him as he wanted her to.

The house felt empty when Jean arrived back. She called out and received silence as her answer in the front hall. She was rather relieved. Though as she moved into the morning-room she could hear a gaggle of voices wafting in through the open french windows from the garden. Freida, Aunt Dizzy in the usual hot pants, Christopher, Fergus, Ivan and Mr Harcourt were all sitting in a circle on chairs arranged around Freida's table, which was overflowing with plates and mugs and a coffee percolator, which threatened to topple over. There was an immediate silence as soon as Jean appeared. Freida and Aunt

Dizzy were looking decidedly guilty, as everyone stared Jean's way apart from Christopher, who was examining his bare right foot, having angled his leg so that his toes were inches away from his flushed face.

'Lady!' Freida called. 'We hadn't expected you back so soon!'

'Plotting?' Jean asked.

'Murder. We're going to poison you, no, bludgeon you to death and then leave you soaking in a bath of water, which will be used afterwards to nourish the garden once your corpse has been hauled away.'

'Slut.'

Christopher, lowering his leg, sniggered. Uncle Fergus whinnied. Mr Harcourt looked decidedly ill at ease, sitting stiffly in his suit and tie balancing a cup and saucer on his knees. He cast Jean a confused, slightly terrified glance then looked away.

'I do apologize, Mr Harcourt,' Jean said as she moved across the grass. 'I didn't intend to leave you alone with this rabble. I had an urgent appointment. Has Christopher been looking after you?'

She glared blackly at Christopher and then pointedly turned her gaze on Fergus. Fergus didn't notice, as he was smiling in an affectionate manner at Aunt Dizzy. He was wearing bright yellow trousers and what looked like a Hawaiian shirt with short sleeves. His pale, hairless arms seemed quite devoid of flesh.

'We were all enjoying a lovely chat about the last war, Jean,' Aunt Dizzy suddenly said with noticeable deceit splashed across her face. 'And television programmes. I'd planned to sleep in, but one must be sociable with a new guest at hand.'

'*Must* one?'

Jean, still standing and irritated, glanced to her left and noticed the top of Mrs Meiklejohn's head, so close to the dividing wall that it was more than likely that the woman had been eavesdropping.

'Good morning, Mrs Meiklejohn!' Jean called, so loudly that everyone jumped. 'How are you coping with this awful heatwave?'

There was no response. The head lowered itself from sight. There were rapid footsteps along her path, followed by the slamming of her door. A flock of sparrows rose up from Mrs Meiklejohn's roof and scattered like storm-tossed leaves.

'Bloody woman. I hope none of you were talking out of turn,' Jean said. 'The Lady Maggot was listening.'

Christopher exchanged a look with his father, who frowned and carefully took up his cup and saucer, placing it on the pile of dirty dishes on the table. Everyone remained silent. Aunt Dizzy pretended to brush crumbs from her purple hot pants and bare legs. Frieda suddenly laughed, then stopped.

'Whoops!' she said.

Unseen and unheard and indoors, Mrs Meiklejohn headed as fast as her short legs would carry her through her spotlessly clean kitchen and into her hall, picking up the telephone, tapping out a number and, while waiting for a reply, gazing with satisfaction at a huge, still-life oil painting which she was convinced was valuable and one day wished to present on *Antiques Roadshow*.

'Nellie?' she said. 'It's me. I have some news. You won't like it. I don't wish to alarm you unduly, but you should know. Now . . .'

Her usually loud voice, as she related what she had heard, descended slowly into a rapid, conspiratorial whisper. The knuckles of her hand turned white as she clutched the receiver of the telephone. Spit flew from her lips, adhering to the mouthpiece of the telephone like tiny globules of benign acid.

FIFTEEN

A black cat sits beside a flower-bed on the dry, yellowing grass in Jean's garden. It crouches forward, sniffing at a particular small area of freshly dug earth, on top of which have been inserted two ice-lolly sticks, stapled together in the shape of a small cross. It is just after sunrise. The cat begins to pat at the earth with a paw and then in a not uncommon feline movement pushes at the earth, which is loose, until a small portion of fur appears. The cat inches forward, still a little suspicious but its senses telling it that here is food. Pushing further at the tiny grave, the cat exposes the withering corpse of the field mouse Christopher has buried there. Delicately, with its teeth, the cat picks up the body and stands to its feet, staring around the garden with widened yellow eyes. Then in one silken movement it turns and runs across the grass towards the rear, leaping with ease up to the top of the wall. Dropping the furry bundle, the cat touches it gently with a seemingly incurious paw until, squatting, it takes the corpse again into its mouth and bites down satisfactorily. The crunching sound as the bones of the body snap is quite loud in the quiet of the warm early morning.

Mrs Meiklejohn, quite unaware of this, is eating her own breakfast of pre-soaked home-made muesli and milk, sitting on a deckchair just outside her back door. Minus her teeth, which she has not yet inserted into her mouth owing to a small ulcer that has not quite healed, she sucks gingerly on a spoonful of cereal and gazes with reptilian eyes at the horizon of the sky, hoping that it might rain but knowing there is little possibility. And as she carefully eats she listens for any sounds from next door, ready to scuttle indoors should anyone appear or call out. She has promised Nellie Harcourt to report anything untoward regarding the goings-on next door. Nellie Harcourt, in turn, is to put in a quiet word at her church to allow Mrs Meiklejohn access to join the flock of the Loving Souls for Jesus, Golders Green Division.

A lone pigeon is perched on the roof of Mrs Meiklejohn's house, unseen, close to the edge, directly above Mrs Meiklejohn's head. The pigeon silently ruffles its feathers. Angling its head sideways to peer up at the sky, it then turns to walk up to the pinnacle of the roof. As it does so it ejects several globules of soft white faeces, one of which is jettisoned out over the edge of the guttering and, as there is not even a slight breeze, the globule plummets directly into the bowl of muesli and milk. Mrs Meiklejohn, at that precise moment, is peering to her right, lifting her head slightly so that she can see whether or not Jean Barrie's french windows are open. She does not notice the addition to her breakfast, so concentrated is she on ascertaining that there is no movement on the other side of the wall. She does not hear the plopping sound the fallen faeces makes in her bowl. After a second or two, having satisfied herself that the french windows next door are still closed, she lifts another spoonful of breakfast to her pursed lips and sucks.

Only Jean and Mr Harcourt are awake. She has got into the habit of taking him an early cup of tea and biscuits, which, he has told her, he deeply appreciates. He is a rather formal man, in manners as well as in speech. Jean pauses, in the act of leaving the room, hoping to chat, for Mr Harcourt is sitting up in bed in his red-and-white striped pyjamas examining one of Ivan's tin toys, which Ivan had been showing him the evening before and left behind.

'Isn't that sweet!' she exclaims, stifling the urge to laugh.

'I had one of these when I was a child,' Mr Harcourt responds.

'Did you *really*?'

'Isn't it extraordinary what triggers memory? I had entirely forgotten I had one of these toys. This is a replica, so I'm told. But it looks exactly the same as far as I can recall.'

The toy is a green-and-brown painted tin mountain through which, at its peak, protrudes a thin length of angled wire on which is attached a small red aeroplane. Around the mountain and through tiny tunnelled gaps travels a miniature train in the opposite direction to which the plane whirls in circles. Mr Harcourt, glancing up with a grin, turns the key, releases a lever and holds up the toy for Jean to admire. His face is a study in constrained delight.

Jean thought Mr Harcourt a trifle simple-minded yet she had warmed to him. He was obviously deeply fond of Christopher and was, to all appearances, a devoted father.

'Mr Harcourt . . .' Jean said, then stopped.

'Sit down,' he said. 'It would be pleasant to have a chat. I am so grateful to you, Miss Barrie, for allowing me to stay, near Christopher. I must admit I was quite upset when Nell . . . Mrs Harcourt, forced him to leave. She takes no notice of me, of course. Hasn't done for most of our married life. My opinions matter little.'

Jean, still in her nightdress and dressing-gown, sat on a chair she'd brought up from the front reception room and which Mr Harcourt used to sit on in contemplation. He also spent a great deal of his time reading a London encyclopaedia, alone in his room but with the door left open, during the day while Christopher was out. He had problems walking and preferred to be indoors.

'Christopher seems perfectly happy here,' Mr Harcourt said.

Jean nodded. 'I've tried to make him feel at home. Your wife . . . Mrs Harcourt has not changed her mind? About him? Oh dear, that's a silly thing to say, after you . . .'

Mr Harcourt placed the tin toy down beside him on the bed. He stared at it and not at Jean as he responded. He shrugged rather tiredly.

'She never wanted Christopher. I'm afraid she's made that clear to him all his life. Forgive my bluntness. I love my son, Miss Barrie. I love him without reserve. Many would condemn me for confessing that I have never minded his, shall we say, close friendship with Fergus. It took me a while to accept it, and that wasn't easy. I guessed, long before my wife found out, what was going on. Well, there was little, in fact, going on. Fergus is quite moral, in his way.'

'You speak about it so calmly.'

'Years of practice, observing Nellie's particular excesses. I was, I'm rather ashamed to admit, *relieved* when she decided I had to go as well. She has all her church friends, dozens of them. I would never have left her, you see. It's made me old before my time putting up with her all these years. We married late. Christopher came along late. I took care of him myself, mostly, when I could. Mrs Harcourt ignored him when she could.'

'How awful. Really.'

'My wife is not a monster. She's just – oh, how can I put it? – over-convinced that her form of religion is the only way she, or anyone, should live. There are reasons for it, but I've no desire to talk about those. One shouldn't necessarily talk about the past. It makes no difference, anyway, going over that which is gone.'

'I know. I know that only too well,' Jean said quietly.

'I'd like to take Christopher across Europe. I've thought about it for some time. Years. Just the two of us. I fear I've left it too late. He's utterly attached, devoted to my brother-in-law. They seem to fit together. In the last day or so I have never seen Christopher so happy, so contented, as he is here and now. I grew up in a strictly conventional way. I want him to find the happiness I was never allowed or offered. Fergus may well provide that. He's a good man. A little eccentric but basically good and kind. He'll provide. For Christopher. My son's an unusual boy. No, young man. It's his birthday in a week or so.'

'I didn't realize!'

Mr Harcourt glanced up at her and quickly looked away.

'Well no,' he said very slowly. 'He never told you. Look, if it is any imposition at all, my being here, then do say. I could easily book into a hotel. I may travel soon. I've been abroad so infrequently. Nellie never wanted to leave London. I'd rather like to visit Rome. Australia attracts. On my own, I imagine. Christopher would not wish to leave his . . . leave Fergus. Not now.'

'Perhaps you could all three travel together?'

Mr Harcourt shook his head. 'No, I don't think that would be ideal. I would like to see Christopher settled before I left.'

Again he looked up at her and was about to say something more, but instead he simply shook his head and smiled. The rims of his eyes had turned red.

Freida had sold her house, receiving the asking price which she had held out for.

'I'm a rich bitch, Lady!' she told Jean. 'Well, richer. I'd suggest we celebrate but you are far too . . . *busy* with the Hibbert boy.'

'Enough of the "boy" if you don't mind. He's in Zurich.'

'Well, he is. A boy I mean. Never imagined it'd go this far. You've surprised me, I'll give you that. He's a rather tasty piece of chicken.'

A family of five had bought the house. Freida did hear from the agent that she could have held out longer and been offered more.

'Glad to be rid, Jean, to tell the truth. You know, I quite fancy somewhere close to Brighton. A little haven beside the sea. You gave me the idea, years ago. I might pop down in a few weeks, have a scout round. Fancy coming? You may feel the need by then.'

'What?'

'Never mind. Come on, go put something girlish on and we'll go out for lunch. My treat. I fancy lobster. Huge, pink, dripping-with-butter lobster. Two. I feel the need right now to suck some sweet white flesh. Oh my, *what* am I saying?'

'What do you want to do for your birthday, sugar plum?' Freida asked. They had each enjoyed a brie salad and crisp white wine – having decided to eat locally and not finding a seafood venue in the high street – and now walked from the restaurant down to the end of the street and across into Regent's Park. The day had turned a little cooler with a few scattered clouds hovering in the white sky, though it was still far too warm. They'd entered the park near the mosque, which Freida hated as she claimed it was ugly architecture and offensive to all those with loose morals. She enjoyed glaring at anyone who entered as she marched past. Finding a bench near the boating lake, Jean had begged to sit beneath the shade of an oak tree. The sun was strong and she found it uncomfortable. They were not wearing hats.

'What have you planned?' Jean asked.

Freida snorted. 'Absolutely nothing, Lady. Zilch.'

'Liar.'

'Honest! I am as honest as the day is cold,' she said, fanning her face with a newspaper someone had left on the bench.

'Peaceful,' Jean mused. 'I'd like a peaceful day sipping gin and lime juice.'

'Is Christopher's father going to stay?'

'For a while. We had a chat this morning. He's a gentle, rather sad man. Thoughtful. He seems simple-minded, but I'm not sure. I like him.'

'You like *everyone*,' Freida said. 'Lady Jean the Tolerant. That's your weakness. You're too bloody *nice*. And impulsive.'

'*Am* I?'

'Doo Lally's announced she's going to slow down, did she tell you? She's not been herself lately. She does look a mite peaky.'

Jean shook her head. Across from them a family were playing an impromptu game of lawn tennis. The father was showing his young son how to hold the ball and how to twist it as he made a serve with his racket. He had powerful, muscular legs and arms and a cleft chin.

'No more late nights, Doo Lally said,' Freida went on. 'She's just bought a hundredweight of vitamins and minerals. Lectures Fergus on his slothful ways. Wants to take up aerobics again. Silly old tart. I do love her. She's really got it in for Ivan. I sense trouble.'

Ivan had taken to sitting upstairs for hours in his rooms, now reading English history and attempting to write a definitive book on golf. He had bought a small, second-hand typewriter, and the sound of it drifted down the stairs in the afternoons when Aunt Dizzy took a rest. She and Ivan had had words, nearly fallen out over the noise, and Jean suspected that the disagreement hadn't ended there.

166

'Birthday?' Freida suddenly said.

'What?'

'You haven't really said. What you'd like to do.'

'As I said. Just stay at home. Drink gin. I enjoy the others being about the house. It's like . . . family.'

'Well, you could take up knitting. No, petit point. You could sit petit pointing cushion covers in an old rocking-chair. Homilies, framed for the walls. They'd hang well beside Doo Lally's dreary paintings. *There's No Place Like Home. Bless This Our Peaceful Dwelling.* You could join the Women's Institute if it still exists. Bake scones and chocolate cake and have tea parties. Tupperware. Announce plans for a knitathon for the poor . . .'

'Oh, do shut up. I am not in the mood.'

Freida fell silent for only a minute.

'I met someone in a bar a few nights ago,' she said. 'Wants me to go and live with her in a condo in Chicago, if you please. Just came out with it. Come to Chicago with me. You'd love it! My ex-husband would adore you!'

'So when are you leaving?'

'Jean! I told her no. I have to remain in London, I said airily, to take care of my dear, sweet great-aunt who has filled her house with human oddities and threatens to become old. Why do Americans find me so irresistible?'

'I'll be fifty-eight,' said Jean.

'I know, dearest. Rotten, isn't it?'

Freida moved closer and slid her arm through Jean's.

'Two old ducks,' she said, 'quacking our way to senility.'

The following two days were dominated by domestic trivia. Freida, having agreed to stay on at the house indefinitely but with Brighton in mind for the future, suggested they tidy or clear the reception room opposite her bedroom.

'I would like more space, Lady,' she told Jean. 'I could entertain my occasional lapses into sexual deviation in there. You can't move, right now, with all Doo Lally's paintings stacked up. At least she's stopped buying them. No taste whatsoever. Money to burn.'

Most of the artwork Jean had insisted be stored in the room, away from the stairs and the morning-room and the hallways, where Aunt Dizzy had left and forgotten about them. Jean, Freida and Christopher spent mornings clearing the room, washing down the walls, carrying boxes of books and old videos and small pieces of furniture as well as paintings upstairs to the pull-down stairs that led up into the roof space above Ivan's rooms. Ivan was spending time at the British Library. With a borrowed card he was researching golf clubs and the changing state of the game, something Aunt Dizzy had been loudly vocal about.

'The height of damned mediocrity,' she'd scoffed. 'A boring subject for a bloody boring man.' As she never said such things to his face, Ivan was quite unaware of her animosity towards him. Aunt Dizzy was researching, she said, health farms. 'So I can get away from this den of boredom,' Jean overheard her telling Christopher. She slept a great deal during the day. She was often withdrawn and pensive.

Anthony telephoned from Zurich. His wife was not contesting their divorce. He couldn't sleep for thinking about Jean.

'I'll be ready and able to marry you sooner than we expect,' he told Jean.

'*We?*'

'You will marry me. There's no question about it.'

'*Will* I?'

'I have to stay another couple of nights. The damned author's being the usual mix of ego and hysterical complaint.'

'I miss you,' Jean told him.

'I love you,' Anthony replied.

They talked for over an hour. Freida kept moving back and forth across the hall from her room to the half-emptied reception room, blowing kisses and wearing less and less clothing until she eventually appeared clad only in bright scarlet frilly knickers, posing in the hall with a long-stemmed rose held carefully between her teeth. Christopher appeared shortly after that with the Hoover and commenced to busy himself noisily with it in the morning-room, until Jean shouted for him to stop. Mr Harcourt sat out in the garden with Ivan, who was showing him and reading aloud from articles in his stack of *National Geographics*. Aunt Dizzy, as usual, was upstairs resting. She had begun to worry Jean a little: she'd become too quiet and did not always appear for breakfast. Forsaking her brightly coloured garb, including the endless pairs of hot pants, she had taken to dressing in long, silken ancient dresses and shuffling about the house in fluffy slippers, usually with ice cubes wrapped in tea towels held to her head. The heat was getting at her, she said, quite cheerfully, when Jean asked if she was unwell. She kept making the odd acerbic remark, mostly about Ivan Fitzpatrick, deriding him to everyone behind his back. Christopher and Fergus failed to interest her in Scrabble or accompanying them on their constant outings when Christopher wasn't up at the library. It was a while before Jean started to take notice of the change in Aunt Dizzy, involved as she was in taking care of Mr Harcourt and Ivan. Both of them seemed incapable of taking care of themselves, to attend to laundry or cleaning the bathroom or the kitchen after bathing or attempting to prepare meals, tasks which, Jean suspected, had previously been done for them.

'I'm a barrel of bounce, a festoon of frivolity, Jean,' Aunt

Dizzy stated one morning as she came slowly down the stairs, half undressed and wig in disarray, long after everyone else had finished breakfast. Her tone of voice did not convince.

Anthony arrived at the house after three days, straight from the airport, dishevelled and laden with duty-free, dropping everything as Jean answered the door and throwing his arms around her as if they'd been forced apart for several decades. At ten thirty in the morning Jean found herself in bed with him, eagerly returning the passion he exhibited with such astonishing depth as if she *was* in love with him. They spent the better part of an entire day lying beneath a silk sheet, entwined and uninhibited for the first time, Jean going downstairs for coffee and snacks like the bedraggled aftermath of sexual indulgence. She went with him back to his apartment. She had extra keys cut so that he could come and go from the house whenever he chose. They went dancing late at night and ate out.

Ivan and Mr Harcourt started to go out together to one of the local pubs in the evenings, usually straight after dinner. Freida had begun to accompany Fergus and Christopher to night-clubs and to exhibitions during the day. Ivan rarely appeared during the day except at mealtimes, bleary-eyed and filled with enthusiasm for his creative efforts on his typewriter, the noise of which continued unabated. Aunt Dizzy's complaints continued. She slept, or said she slept. She sat alone in the front reception room or sometimes in Freida's room playing solitaire with cards or watching television, rarely venturing out of the house. She acted cheerful, resigned to her new solitary ways.

'I am quite content, Jean. You mustn't fuss, it's irritating,' she kept saying whenever Jean asked if she needed anything.

•

Jean had come back to the house having spent the night in Covent Garden with Anthony. It was just past eleven o'clock in the morning, only a few days before her birthday. She had suspicions that something had been organized; Christopher kept dropping hints.

Dirty breakfast dishes were strewn all about the kitchen and on every surface in the morning-room. Freida, Ivan, Christopher and his father were out in the garden. A hose-pipe ban having just been lifted, Christopher was watering the garden, with his father seemingly offering unheeded but humorous directions, as Christopher was loudly sniggering. Freida and Ivan sat chatting to each other, Ivan even laughing occasionally and slapping his thighs. Coffee mugs sat on the grass like featureless china gnomes. Jean stood silently watching from the comparative shade of the morning-room. It was a brilliant white-hot day already. For a few moments a feeling of deep satisfaction touched her. She had not drunk more than anyone else for weeks. She was sleeping deeply. She awoke in the mornings with voices reaching her from other parts of the house, sounds which brought mild expectation and a cheerfulness that pleased her. She did not even mind being at Anthony's apartment any longer.

Aunt Dizzy was nowhere to be seen. She was not in the kitchen where she sometimes sat once she'd descended from her room, sipping mugs of lemon or herbal tea and contemplating the plastic containers of vitamin and mineral tablets she carried about with her inside a leather toiletries bag. She had started offering tablets to everyone – everyone except Ivan – but rarely getting takers. Jean checked the front reception room and Freida's room. Both were empty. She did not hurry up the stairs, imagining Aunt Dizzy to be asleep still or possibly soaking in the bath, which she often did now in the mornings, to cool herself, she had said.

The bathroom was empty. Several pairs of Christopher's

stylish designer-label underpants lay drying on the electric wall heater. Jean picked them up, folding them, switching off the heater. The door leading from the bathroom into Aunt Dizzy's room was locked when she tried to open it. She knocked.

'Auntie?' she called. There was no reply. Jean passed through the other door – almost always left open – into Christopher's bedroom and laid the underwear on his neatly made bed. The house was too quiet, she thought suddenly. It seems to be holding its breath. Christopher had told her that he believed Acacia Road was a living, breathing entity so many times she found herself, at odd moments when distracted, thinking as though she believed him.

Aunt Dizzy's door from the hall was closed but unlocked. Jean opened the door slowly and peered in. The curtains were still drawn. The room smelt fusty. For a second she let her eyes adjust to the gloom.

'Auntie?'

On the floor beside her bed Aunt Dizzy lay on her side with one arm thrown out, clutching a bottle of vitamin E tablets. Jean found herself staring at the bottle for what must have been thirty seconds before she pushed the door fully open and stepped inside.

'There you are,' Jean whispered. 'It's gone eleven o'clock, Auntie. Time to get dressed. This won't do, will it?'

Moving slowly across the room, Jean knelt down at Aunt Dizzy's side. Without thinking, she removed the bottle of tablets from Aunt Dizzy's hand and held the bottle up to her chest.

Gazing down at the open, vacant eyes staring upwards, Jean's eyes were filled with love and with the overwhelmingly painful understanding that had come to her as soon as she'd stepped into the room, that Elizabeth had gone away and would never be coming back.

SIXTEEN

After the funeral everyone except Jean and Anthony walked back to Acacia Road, where Freida had organized drinks and sandwiches. Anthony took Jean by taxi to his apartment, where she suddenly wished to be alone with him. It had been a quiet, non-religious service at the local church in the high street. A little impersonal but civilized and calm. Jean insisted that the others sit with her, around her, to be close. There had only been about twelve people in the church. Two or three had come from the Mayfair hotel and an elderly couple Aunt Dizzy had known drove up from Hampshire. It shocked Jean that so few had been there. Cedric Hyde, Aunt Dizzy's sometime paramour, sat behind her and wept but spoke only briefly before and after. Several days before, Jean had telephoned a contact number in California and left a message, asking for Elizabeth's son to call back immediately. He hadn't called, nor appeared, but had sent an enormous, ostentatious wreath, so large it took three men to carry it from the hearse. When he had not returned her call Jean had telephoned a second time, again leaving a message, that Rupert Barrie's mother had passed away. Aunt Dizzy, while she'd been alive, had not heard from him for two decades.

There was an enormous number of flowers and wreaths. One shaped like a cross from Mr Alder at the hotel which would have, Jean knew, made Aunt Dizzy laugh or produce one of her pointed comments. Mr Alder did not put in an appearance. Flowers had arrived at the house from all over the country and New York. Jean also telephoned William but had not spoken to him for long. He said nothing at all about his father nor asked after him. William had offered to fly across – 'I could possibly find a day's window, but things are hectic over here, Jean,' he'd said – and she'd responded coldly, rudely, suggesting he not put himself out, that flowers would be more suitable anyway. She told him little. There was, in fact, little to tell. Elizabeth had apparently suffered several seizures during the night. The last one had ended her life. She would not have suffered unduly, Jean was earnestly informed by her GP. Aunt Dizzy's face, when Jean found her, *had* been composed and peaceful. It was almost as though Aunt Dizzy had simply lain down on the floor to sleep. Jean sat beside her for more than half an hour before going downstairs.

Christopher wept bitterly at the news and continued to do so off and on for several days. He spent most of that time not with Fergus but with his father, walking in Regent's Park. Fergus came and went from the house with a genuinely doleful expression, dressed in a variety of black suits and ties. He sat beside Christopher at the funeral, Mr Harcourt on the other side. Both of them held Christopher's hands. Jean sat with her eyes closed throughout. She was not praying as others thought she might be but remembering Aunt Dizzy as she would always remember her, and sometimes she smiled and let out small sounds of recollected humour which she managed to disguise by coughing delicately into a handkerchief. When the service was concluded, the coffin was driven to a crematorium, attended only by employees of the funeral parlour, where Aunt Dizzy's remains were cremated. She had left strict, explicit instructions in her will that this was to be done, not explaining why. Almost all of her money and possessions she left to Jean.

There was a late addition, made to her will only a few weeks before, that five thousand pounds be given to Christopher Harcourt.

Once she and Anthony arrived at his apartment Jean immediately began to drink heavily. He said nothing but stood leaning against the frame of the kitchen door watching her. She sat on a high stool at his breakfast bar and rapidly downed one straight gin after another, recalling in her mind the last night of the Albert Hall concerts and the half-bottle of gin Aunt Dizzy had taken with her, wrapped in several layers of brown paper. She had guarded the gin as if it was priceless, was so secretive about it and at every opportunity when they were alone urged Jean to take a few sips. To fortify her, she said. Jean obstinately refusing, as she rarely drank anything but bottled water before a performance.

'You're no fun,' Aunt Dizzy had complained. 'You're no fun at all.' She began to drink the gin herself and fell asleep twice, sitting with the children in the second row while Jean was on stage.

'She didn't want to go,' Jean suddenly said into the silence of the kitchen. Anthony did not respond. For Jean spoke as if she was talking aloud to herself, not even glancing his way.

'She refused, afterwards, just refused point-blank. I am *not* being dragged down to bloody Wales, Jean, she said. The first time she had *ever* sworn in my hearing. The gin, probably. And that was that. She didn't come. I was so angry at her. I was angry at her and angry at William because *he* couldn't even be bothered to be there at all. Bastard. Prick. But I took the others. I drove them all down there, to . . .'

She stopped. Her hands began to shake uncontrollably and the glass slipped from her and fell to the polished wooden floor, shattering into several pieces. Jean pushed herself off the stool and stood there, bent down, staring at the glass. 'It was me, it was *me*,' she muttered. She started to slap at her face, then laughed. Anthony swiftly crossed the room and took hold of her, steadying her as she straightened. Taking both her hands he led her from the kitchen down the short hallway to the bedroom. He undressed her, helping her on to the bed and enfolding the duvet around her. The room was air-conditioned and cool. He half lay beside her but did not touch her. Jean lay back against the pillows and stared at him with a puzzled expression as if she was not certain who he was.

In a few minutes she was deeply asleep.

She slept for almost half an hour but woke suddenly, crying out, immediately bursting into tears and as suddenly stopping and gazing about her, drawing up her hands to rub at her face. She started to whisper, then to mutter something angrily, but he could not hear what she was saying. Tears began to course down her face, gathering at the base of her chin.

'Talk to me,' he said. 'Talk to me, Jean. Please.'

Jean shuddered. Anthony waited, gazing with gentleness at her face. She would not look at him. She turned away her head and stared at the wall.

'She didn't wish to go and that saved her life,' Jean whispered.

And as she continued her voice gathered strength. Her voice grew louder, yet she spoke in a flat, unemotional tone as though she was still talking to herself, as if she were alone in the room.

Jean had pleaded with Aunt Dizzy to join her, Jared, Gemma and their grandparents that night, to drive down to the cottage in Wales directly after the final concert at the Albert Hall. Jean had decided to go, just as she made all her decisions, impulsively and refused to be persuaded otherwise. Isobelle, Jean's mother, had been totally against the idea. She'd thought it preposterous.

Jean wasn't in her right mind. It was too far. It was too cold. Despite the euphoria that Jean was overwhelmed by, drunk from the success she knew she'd created, she had shouted at Isobelle, eventually, before they'd even joined the motorway. Jean's father tried to intervene and Jared began clapping and shouting for them to shut the hell up, and for several miles, as Jean continued to drive, bitter argument and recrimination cut back and forth and the concert was not mentioned once, and no one even congratulated her. So Jean drove. She drove furiously, singing to herself in the long silences that eventuated until Isobelle began again, then again to try to change Jean's mind so she would turn back. The night was clear and cold and there was to be a heavy frost before dawn – that would have nothing to do with what was to happen. Jean's mind was filled with sounds of applause and people down in front of her standing to their feet, faces smiling, and there were some who'd cried out and others who did not wish her to leave the stage, back to the dressing-room and to Aunt Dizzy who was there flourishing her almost empty bottle of gin. And Jean had thought, as she stood still on the stage: I shall take them all down to Wales, to where I played and ran and sang as a child and grandfather taught me how to fish. I want to be there with them, with Mother and Father and the children. Just us. Damn William for not being with us. Damn Aunt Dizzy.

Isobelle had grown resigned and almost calm by the time they stopped to eat, and of course the family were never less than loving in public. The second part of the journey was warily peaceful. Yet still no one, not even Jared, mentioned the concert. He and Gemma both fell asleep. Jean's father Edward joined her in the front and sat there occasionally chatting about nothing in particular and making certain she took the correct motorway turn-off.

Isobelle had also fallen asleep when Jean took a wrong turning and they were lost, for a while, during which time Jean and her father giggled like children, imagining what Isobelle would say if she were awake and knowing Jean had got them lost after refusing to turn back. And Edward, her dear, beloved, worshipped father, had begun to tell her in his hesitant way that it had been the proudest moment of his long and happy life to witness his only daughter there in front of that distinguished audience. To have seen her, he'd said, being applauded with such huge emotion and respect had touched his heart more deeply than anything else he could remember. He was quite happy to return to the cottage just for a day or two. He understood, he had told her, why. He understood that it was a place Jean had also been gloriously happy in as a child, where he, too had spent so many special times when he was young. It was fitting.

Sometime, while he was speaking, Jean's mother had woken from her nap. Eventually, as she must have heard most of her husband's unrehearsed speech, she leant forward and awkwardly kissed Jean on the side of her head, yet at the same time warning her not to take her eyes off the road. Then she sat for the duration of the journey mostly in silence, yet sometimes commenting that she recognized this or that out the window, then worrying aloud that none of them had brought toothbrushes and the bed-linen in the cottage would need to be aired and they would have to use the gas cylinders stored in the basement. There'd be no electricity until they could telephone someone the following morning. Gemma and Jared remained asleep. Isobelle laughed when Gemma started to snore; Gemma had once sworn that she never snored. Jean hummed to herself and drove more slowly now that Isobelle was awake and did not get them lost again, exchanging small secretive smiles with her father.

Jean dropped them off at the top of the track, which wound down through dense woodland to the cottage. She wanted to drive on for a while, she told her father, to calm herself or she would never sleep. He had the keys and could let the others in. Isobelle was not happy at the prospect of having to walk down the track but said little in protest. Jean watched them in the rear-view mirror as she drove off. Gemma was hugging her grandmother, saying something to her which made Isobelle laugh. Jared was beating his arms against himself. Their breath frosted in the cold air. Jared was to turn nineteen that year. Gemma was two years younger.

Her father was waving as Jean turned a corner and then they were gone from sight. She was never to see them alive again.

She drove for several miles, recognizing, even in the dark that was lightened by a half-moon, places she had been to as a child. Houses and small neglected farm dwellings she had gazed at, walked past, were still there. Picnic areas. A stream where she and her father had first fished and where she had fallen in and ruined a dress she'd hated. It was an isolated area and still was. She drove slowly, savouring the night, encountering little other traffic, for it was by then the early hours of the morning. It was a time Jean enjoyed, being awake when the world around her was resting. Eventually, suddenly tired and heavy-headed, she pulled into the gravelled car park of a hotel she did not recognize, which looked newly built or even unfinished. Lights shone inside. There were several other cars and a van parked across the forecourt. After a few minutes she rested her head against the side window, closing her eyes, the stream of smiling faces and waving arms and the cries of appreciation that had been reverberating inside her head now slowly fading. She would rest for five minutes, she thought, and then return to the cottage. Exhaustion rolled over her.

She was woken by the sound of someone tapping on the window glass and she immediately sat upright in fright, having slipped down into the seat. A woman was staring in at her, a homely face, her head covered by a scarf. It was still dark. Jean had slept for more than an hour.

'I'm sorry! Are you all right, love?' the woman called. Jean wound down the window. 'You must be freezing out here. Look, the hotel isn't open yet, but we've been having an early breakfast. Late night last night, but none of us slept for long. Just noticed you out here! Are you sure you're OK?'

Once Jean had opened her door and stepped out, the woman, short, wide-hipped, plain-featured and concerned, asked her in for some hot soup or coffee. 'You look as if you need *something*,' she said. 'Travelled far?'

Jean found herself following the woman into the hotel, where various people were lounging about on plastic-film-covered armchairs and sofas. A baby was asleep inside a modern plastic carrycot on the deep-pile carpeted floor. No one took a great deal of notice at first, except to nod greetings, apart from a woman who stared rudely, her mouth dropping open. She then nudged the man sitting beside her, whispering to him. The man began to stare. Both grinned. The woman had several teeth missing.

'Never mind this lot,' the woman who'd invited her in said cheerfully. 'I'm Gracie. After Gracie Fields. We're all from up north, just come down yesterday. Had this place built to make our fortune. We're all too wacked right now to care!' and she laughed so loudly Jean involuntarily winced. She was still only half awake. The main reception room, where everyone sat, was warm. There was a large open fireplace piled with glowing, flaming logs and a strong odour of coffee and frying bacon.

'It's so kind of you,' Jean said, rather ineffectually. 'I'm Jean.'

'Sit over by the fire, Jean. Coffee?' Then she added, 'Neville, get your fat arse up off that chair and come and help. You did bugger all yesterday.'

Forgetting the time, Jean had stayed until almost dawn. The hotel owners were a family, a large, extended family, she was told. 'The men are all lazy buggers and us women do all the slogging,' Gracie told her, laughing. Jean was treated as if she was to be their very first guest. She was soon given a plate piled high with fried eggs and sausages and tomatoes, most of which she left. She kept being offered coffee or tea and was fussed over. Each of them included her in idle chat, smiling and laughing. The large imposing Gracie appeared to be in charge. She reminded Jean of Peggy Mount. Jean gave little thought to her own family, probably worrying about her back at the cottage – or not, as she guessed they would have all gone to bed, as utterly exhausted as she was now beginning to feel. She sat basking in the easy-going comfort the others displayed. The woman who had openly stared was Gracie's sister. Jean had been there only twenty minutes before she sidled over and stood nervously fidgeting with a lock of her hair and gazing down at Jean in a slightly disturbing way. Then she said, too rapidly, 'I hope you won't mind, but aren't you Jean Barrie?' and then looked stricken, glancing back into the room.

'I am. For all my sins,' Jean said and smiled as warmly as she could manage to, glancing back at the fire, suddenly embarrassed. Everyone in the room stared at her with varying degrees of interest.

'I knew it! I said to Mervyn as soon as you walked in, that's Lady Jean! Oh, look, I'm such a fan as you wouldn't believe. Got all your records, every one. You signed one for me once. You won't remember.' She turned her head and called, 'It *is* her, Merv, I told you!'

Jean shuddered.

After that it wasn't easy for Jean to get away. Most of the others, even Gracie, didn't seem all that impressed, and Jean suspected a few of them had never heard of her, which was much more comfortable to deal with, when Gracie's sister talked non-stop, breathlessly, as if she was, and had been for years, an intimate friend. In a very short space of time Jean learnt every possible fact about the entire family, from where they'd been born to christenings and weddings to the day poor Mervyn had to wear a ('huge!') colostomy bag after a serious operation – 'down there', the woman confided, leaning forward and loudly whispering, pointing vaguely towards Jean's lap. He had worn the bag for five weeks, much to his shame and was 'not the same man now, if you get what I'm at, poor Merv. He suffered for years.'

When Jean did finally manage to escape, Gracie and her sister came out to wave her off. None of the others followed. Some had fallen asleep. Those who were still awake stood up and shook her hand. The baby was awake and crying loudly but was ignored. Gracie's sister – Jean never learnt her name – warbled on even as Jean made her way over to the car, just as she had done all the time she sat beside Jean on a sofa, smiling confidingly and grinning with the gaps in her teeth every time Jean glanced at her. Jean signed several battered albums, produced from a plastic carrier bag, then an old programme. She baulked at signing Gracie's sister's grubby sweatshirt.

It was growing light as Jean drove back the way she had come. The day promised to be sunny, the sky almost completely clear of cloud, the green quality of the surrounding woodland and pasture rich and refreshing and uplifting as the light brightened. It was so quiet. Jean thought of the days ahead. She yearned for sleep. She was relaxed and sanguine from the company of friendly, ordinary people.

The cottage was still burning fiercely after she had driven down the track and reached it. There were two ancient-looking fire engines, a police car and one ambulance parked outside. There had been another police car up on the road, inside of it two policewomen who had clambered out, rushed over and flagged her down as she turned into the track. Most of the cottage had gone by the time Jean saw it, fallen in on itself, the top floor completely collapsed down on to the ground. Smoke rose in thick dark plumes into the ever-lightening sky. Firemen were still using hoses. On the gravel drive lay five bodies covered in black plastic sheeting. They were not easily identifiable, Jean was eventually to be told. She was spared being shown them until much later. There had been one other male adult who had still been alive but had died, not regaining consciousness, on the way to the nearest hospital, miles away.

Jean remained outwardly calm and in control during the next few weeks, much of which she was never to remember clearly. She was driven to the nearest village, sat in a dark green-painted room for several hours, questioned, drank tea, wept, even slept, was in shock so that the following events passed by as if it were a film she was watching in a darkened cinema. She was driven back up to London in the family car by a policewoman she never thanked. The bodies of Jared, Gemma and her parents were driven back up to London once they had been officially identified. The other two, both males, were never to be identified at all, despite extensive investigation.

Facts were revealed over time with a sensitivity that Jean, even within the greyness of that period, was impressed by. Her parents' bodies had been found bound and gagged in their bedroom underneath the double bed. Jared's body had been found lying on the kitchen floor. He had been severely beaten around the head and was also tied up. Gemma was lying in the hallway downstairs, close to the bodies of the two unidentified males, one who was rushed off by ambulance but who died soon after. It seemed reasonable to assume, Jean was told, that Gemma and the two men were making their way towards the front door when the flames, or smoke, had engulfed them. The remains of two rifles were also found there. The two large gas cylinders in the cottage had, some time after the fire had been deliberately started – by whom no one knew – exploded and escalated the rapid, complete envelopment of the cottage by the fire. There was evidence that the cottage had been occupied for some time, probably by the two men. The local handyman, four miles away, who had been paid to keep a check on the property, eventually confessed to not having been near for over three months. For a time he became a suspect, but was eventually cleared.

The weeks that passed after that morning revealed, along with the facts and suppositions, implications that Jean refused to deal with. Both Gemma and Jared had been sexually assaulted before they had died. Isobelle had also been beaten and had had her right arm broken, facts that Jean banished from her mind for months. There was never to be any full explanation about what happened. Only speculation. Despite the bodies being examined thoroughly, forensic evidence and all the meticulous, detailed investigation and reports, it was never to be known why the events had occurred. Whether the two men were already inside the house when the family had entered remained unknown. There were no witnesses. A local woman, hearing two distinct explosions, reported that to the police from some distance away. There was evidence of violence. Furniture and doors inside the house had been smashed. The case went on for months, speculated about and written about in the press with varying degrees of taste.

Jean was protected from the press to an astonishing degree, protected from television reports and from those who came forward offering her help. The one funeral was held quietly in a small chapel in north London, the details of which were mostly suppressed by Jean's solicitor with the help of the police. Jean was unable to attend. Jared, Gemma and her parents were buried in Scotland on land that Jean's father owned. Jean, with Freida, drove up there much later to inspect the graves. They never went back. Jean created a private fund to pay for the care of the grave site and the small area of land where her father's ancestors had once farmed. For two months Jean remained, secretly, in an exclusive private nursing home, mostly under sedation. William, unable to cope with his grief, eventually flew to New York where he was, almost a year later, to seek divorce. Aunt Dizzy, with Freida's help, had stood by Jean and taken care of everything. Months later Jean absolutely insisted that they were never to speak about what happened, never to talk to her or to others. Any details, even small, that had not been publicly released should remain unspoken. Once Jean was back at Acacia Road she made the decision to give up her singing career entirely, against *all* advice. It was to be a long time before she agreed to attempt an autobiography, then to lose interest and allow Anthony into her life. By then life had become almost bearable because she continued to drink heavily and Freida, never judgemental, remained with her almost constantly until Jean was able to cope on her own.

'Auntie was nothing less than magnificent,' Jean whispered to the wall, still lying on Anthony's bed. 'I never thanked her. Not once. I never wished to talk about it, to anyone. I never have, until now. I never imagined I would. I don't know why I've spoken of it to you.'

She slowly rolled over to face Anthony and, reaching out, pulled him to her, burying her face into his shoulder and clinging to him, breathing in gasps, shuddering every so often. Eventually she drew away.

'I won't talk about it again,' she said, almost whispering. Then she added, 'I must go home. I can't stay here. Will you take me?'

'Of course. I'll call for a cab. You're sure? You can spend the night.'

Jean shook her head. She said nothing else. After a long silence the telephone rang again. It had rung all during the time Jean was speaking, but Anthony ignored it. It was Freida. Anthony talked to her for a long time.

Freida was waiting for them in the morning-room when Jean and Anthony arrived back at the house. She was alone. She stepped across the room and took Jean in her arms and over her shoulder raised her eyebrows at Anthony, and he smiled sadly and shrugged and then nodded, mouthing that he would leave them for a while.

'I'll call back later,' he said in a whisper.

It was Freida who helped Jean upstairs and put her to bed, Jean barely responding. Yet she did not want Freida to leave the room and held on to her for a long time, neither of them speaking. Freida had sent the others out as soon as she'd got through to Anthony and heard that Jean was returning to the house. Freida sat on the bed stroking Jean's hair until she fell asleep. Anthony returned several hours later. He remained there overnight.

They were all gathered downstairs – Ivan and Mr Harcourt, Christopher and Freida and Anthony – when she awoke the following morning. Christopher knocked on her door just after ten.

'I've made breakfast,' he said, carrying in a laden tray. 'Toast. Marmalade. Scrambled egg. One sausage. It's burnt. I've brewed good coffee.'

His face, eyes diverted, was a deep carmine red as he crossed the room to her bed. His large ears, the same colour, were like oval beacons. His hands trembled as he placed the tray down on the table beside her bed. And when she reached out and took both of his hands and pressed them briefly to her lips he did not snigger or say anything at all but stood there gazing away from her, out through the window, his hands still but his features twisted into an expression of terrible pain which he had managed, until then, to conceal.

SEPTEMBER

Autumn has been delayed, the weather forecasters are cheerfully claiming on radio and television. The long summer still
holds court over London, though the heat has lessened. There
have been one or two days of welcomed rain.

The house looks peaceful from the outside. Perhaps it is
asleep, as it is still relatively early in the morning and the day is
to be special. All inside are asleep. On the pinnacle of the slated
roof pigeon and starling and sparrow deposits have set and
hardened into small crusty mounds so that the roof appears to
be grey along the top instead of charcoal black. In Ivan Fitzpatrick's rooms the hidden mural of Jean on the main wall is
slowly beginning to show itself through the layers of applied
paint. Ivan has been examining it. Without mentioning it to Jean
or anyone else, he sits there on awakening and wonders whether
he is discovering a lost masterpiece.

At nine o'clock on this Saturday morning, along Loudoun
Road near by, two women walk close together in deep whispered conversation. They are plotting. Neither Mrs Meiklejohn
nor Nellie Harcourt know that on the same street a long, long
time ago lived a woman called Mary Baker, who eventually
became known as Mrs Meres. It is said that she was the inspiration for Thackeray's scheming and manipulative Becky Sharp.
Nor do the plotting women, who are mostly ignorant of history,
realize that the very ground they walk on was once, in the
Middle Ages, forest and woodland where wild pigs and sows

roamed; that a man called Anthony Babington, who plotted to murder Queen Elizabeth and put Mary, Queen of Scots on to the throne, hid in this same area with his conspirators. Mrs Meiklejohn and Mrs Harcourt have not been, it must be stressed, plotting murder. But they have been plotting, nevertheless, heading towards the house of one of their own conspirators for morning prayers and final discussion on a particular event; an event that Mrs Meiklejohn has gleefully discovered, from eavesdropping, is to occur later in the day.

On the lawn at Acacia Road stands a small, pink-and-white striped marquee. It is more of a tent, rather medieval in its shape: decorative, tapering from the square top and open at the front. Leading down into the garden from the french windows stretches a length of dull-red carpet – pink not being available – all the way to the entrance of the tent. Sitting inside the tent on the grass is the black cat, using its right paw, which it occasionally licks, to wash its face. Beside it, half eaten, lies a dead headless sparrow. The cat enjoys a varied diet.

All is arranged for a modest, brief blessing of Christopher's and Fergus's union. It has been thought that the ceremony, which is also to be, after the blessing, a late celebration of both Jean's and Christopher's birthdays, should go ahead as Aunt Dizzy would have wanted but in an altered form. Weeks have passed. Recent wounds are warily healing. Jean and Freida have been to the grounds of the crematorium and officially laid a plaque in Aunt Dizzy's memory and planted a tree which will, they hope, grow and spread its branches. Eventually the tree should scatter petals of pink blossom down on to the plaque. Elizabeth Barrie's ashes rest inside an urn, now standing unobtrusively in the corner of the Green Room, alongside a vase in which fresh roses are placed at regular intervals. Jean sits in the Green Room in the early mornings, sometimes reading, sometimes just sitting and gazing out through the windows at the all-too-soon-to-be autumnal sky. When she is not taking care of her remaining guests she is usually with Anthony Hibbert, whom she now loves with a quiet but uncertain devotion that few understand. As she makes little effort to look younger than she is and Anthony dresses in an almost juvenile style, he could well be mistaken for her son. Just as Freida could be mistaken, with applied imagination, for a daughter.

The three are often out together, at the theatre or attending an occasional concert at the Festival Hall. Freida, for the time being and since Aunt Dizzy's death, has given up on her promiscuous quest for a soulmate. She has in fact become, surprising herself, rather domestic. She helps Jean take care of Christopher and Ivan and Mr Harcourt, and Fergus when he is at the house. Freida and Jean have discussed asking someone else to move in but do not wish to advertise for fear of inheriting another Fallen Nun. There is the possibility, of course, that Fergus might wish to live at Acacia Road; he is considering the idea, which Jean has suggested to him. But he shall not decide until he and Christopher return from their honeymoon, visiting the Florida Everglades followed by a tour of South Carolina. Fergus has distant relatives in Savannah whom they will visit.

Christopher is alone in his room on the first floor. He is awake now and sitting on the edge of his bed examining his knees, dressed in fresh, newly bought underpants and vest. He has had his hair cut at a stylish male barbershop off Baker Street where Mr Harcourt has an account. He has been fitted for a new suit which now hangs in a sealed polythene bag from the curtain rail. He noticed that his knees were red and possibly a little swollen on awakening, as he spent time on them weeding the flower-beds so they would look tidy on the day. He has also planted several species of daisies in neat rows. Fergus has spent the night at his own apartment off Long Acre so that he and Christopher will both be refreshed and calm on the day. Fergus is to arrive at the house just before noon, when the blessing will immediately take place. Christopher, perhaps unwisely, has sent a card to his mother telling her of the blessing but not when it is to occur. At the bottom of the card he wrote, *I love you, Mother.* Mrs Meiklejohn, through eavesdropping, has of course informed Mrs Harcourt of the date and even the time when the ceremony is to take place and is to be richly rewarded, she has been promised, by Mrs Harcourt as well as by Jesus.

The house creaks. Christopher listens, his head at an angle. He believes the house is waking and that it is happy at the prospect of the day. In the background he is certain he can hear a contented humming, emanating from inside the walls, that implies the house is not only alive but is much more contented than it was when Christopher first moved in. The walls were utterly silent for several days after Aunt Dizzy died. The unused electricity did not chatter, the floorboards did not creak of their own accord, foundations did not shift. He sometimes still hears mice when he creeps downstairs into the kitchen during the night, but he has not set another trap. On the evening of the day Aunt Dizzy was cremated the lights flickered at seven o'clock and then at ten and then at midnight. No one, except for Christopher, noticed. He sits, having ascertained that his knees are merely tender from the time he spent weeding and planting in the garden. He sits and stares at the opposite wall and smiles. A warmth, like a ghost of pleasant promise, immediately passes through him and he continues to smile. His father is running a bath. Murmuring voices reach his hearing coming from the Green Room, where Freida is with Jean.

•

'Happy birthday, Lady.'

'Don't be silly. It was weeks ago.'

'So,' Freida said, 'we never celebrated it. So it's today. And Christopher's, as you well know. As we all decided last week, in the garden. Remember? No secret plans or surprises. Well, almost none. We shall all have a barrel of fun and cry if we want to.'

They sat on cushioned chairs either side of Aunt Dizzy's urn, sipping mugs of coffee that Jean had brewed. They were still dressed in their nightclothes, Jean in pink and Freida in blue. Freida spent the night in Jean's bed, as she did now, occasionally, when Anthony was not at the house. Anthony did not mind, when Jean told him. He is a little jealous, he told Freida, as he thinks Freida is beautiful. Freida told him she was still in mourning for Aunt Dizzy but would probably continue her promiscuous pathway, only with carefully chosen younger women, once the time of mourning was past.

'I've never said until now,' Freida told Jean, 'but I'm ever so relieved you talked to Anthony. About the past. I only wish it had been me you chose to talk to.'

'He told you.'

Freida nodded. 'On the day. He *was* deeply upset. All these years, you keeping it inside you, insisting Doo Lally and I say nothing. It was hard, Lady. Hard for both of us. To stay quiet. Especially for Doo Lally. Edward *was* her only brother.'

'What was it Mr Harcourt said only a while ago? Something about talking of what has gone, that it doesn't solve anything. He's such a sweet man. I'm pleased he's here. I'm pleased you've *all* stayed on. Really.'

'Will you marry Baby Tony?'

Jean shook her head and sipped from her mug. She glanced down at Aunt Dizzy's urn. Reaching out, she touched it with the tips of her fingers. 'He keeps asking, bless him. It's become a contest to see who will give in first. He shan't win. I suppose I do love him. That's enough.'

'This is too droll. Tutu droll, if you like. Today should be *fun*. Fred the Frock – no sorry, *Father* O'Connell – is hugely looking forward to it. Especially the meal. You know he actually cancelled two appointments so he could spend more time with us? He adores me, of course. Not often he gets to conduct a blessing in *St John's Wood*. Brixton, yes, Even Balham. Putney, once. Lewisham. On Clapham Common he betrothed two ancient fairies in matching wheelchairs.'

'Yes all right, Freida. Now when are the flowers being delivered? And the cake? Will that be ready?'

Mrs Meiklejohn stands in her kitchen and is preparing honeyed ham and watercress sandwiches. She is smiling, a rare phenomenon. Her smile pushes up the pouches beneath her eyes so that it appears she doesn't have any. Guests are to arrive at exactly eleven forty-five and must not be late. Only five of them, six altogether including herself, she's been told. The bluntly worded placards, red paint still gleaming, stand in a row in the front hall. Mrs Meiklejohn has brought out her very best china from the glass-fronted cabinet she has owned since 1929. She has washed each cup and saucer lovingly in the kitchen sink and set each out to dry on a thick towel in her airing cupboard. She trims the crusts of the prepared sandwiches and inspects the chocolate cake, covered by cling-film, to see that it does not have any dents in its perfectly circular form. There are store-bought scones, whipped cream and jam. There are two plates of cocktail sausages on sticks and diced fruit in bowls with small, delicate, solid-silver spoons. She gazes out through her kitchen window, nibbling on a watercress stem, her eyes resting on the top of the hideous pink-and-white tent next door. As far as she can ascertain there is no activity going on *there* yet. Knowing Jean Barrie as she does, there will be a horde of invited guests, dozens of them, even the chance of several distinguished people, if people from the entertainment world could be classed as distinguished. She has convinced herself that there will be a huge number of guests and so informed Nellie Harcourt as if it was a fact. There'll be a small orchestra, too, she stated, again having convinced herself that there will be one and relating it as an overheard fact. Fireworks, she'd heard some time ago, would be a feature. And a barbecue meal on the lawn. Deplorable, all of it, only weeks after a bereavement. No respect. Mrs Meiklejohn shivers, there in her spartan, pristine kitchen. She has *never* liked the Barrie clan. She regards this as simple dislike and not envy or resentment. Mrs Meiklejohn does not regard herself to be envious of anyone. She does still resent her husband for abandoning her. Yet soon she will be a fully fledged member of Nellie's church. Life will become busy, filled with happy days and joy and visitors who will bring respect, and she will belong to a select group of good, moral people.

Jean grieved for Aunt Dizzy. Talking to Anthony about the past made no difference to the pain of losing Elizabeth Barrie. She had not, of course, expected it to and she still did not understand just why she had spoken to Anthony in such a candid way. There were any number of reasons, such as shock. Aunt Dizzy's room had so far been left as it was on the day – or night – that she'd died, but Jean planned to convert the room for Fergus, so that even if he did not wish to live at Acacia Road he could use the room and give both Christopher and himself more space, more privacy. Christopher, she knew, wished for the latter. Jean had seriously considered having other guests, semi-permanent or casual. There *were* distant relatives that Fergus spoke of, in

America, who would, he claimed with his peculiar naïvety, be charmed to stay in a normal English household when they visited London.

The gap Aunt Dizzy left had not narrowed and probably never would. The absence of her voice, her little ways, were things Jean noticed every day, and when she was feeling especially tired and vulnerable the quietness of where Aunt Dizzy had been seemed so deep and abiding that it brought pain. She could never be replaced, never be removed from the house, just as the rest of the family, with the exception of William, could never be replaced or removed. She began to think about Brighton at odd moments, about buying a house down there.

Mr Alder had telephoned to apologize for not having been at the funeral. He'd offered no excuse. Letters had come, including a card from William that had at least made up, in a minuscule way, for his not bothering to fly back. Though, as Freida had pointed out, the writing on the card, she was certain, had not been William's; it had been a feminine hand. Jean spent two weeks unable to leave the house at all, and for a few days she became obsessed with the notion that it had all been a mistake, that Elizabeth was not dead and was recovering somewhere in a hospital. As Ivan had kept expecting to see his late wife, Jean hoped she would see Elizabeth coming down the stairs or languishing in the garden wearing hot pants. Saying nothing to anyone, Jean wandered the rooms *looking* for her aunt when no one else was about. Then, one morning, she awoke and the small obsession had simply left her. She thoroughly cleaned Aunt Dizzy's room, leaving the same linen on the bed and not disturbing the arrangement of her aunt's possessions, drawing back the curtains and opening the windows. Anthony stayed close to her for that time, sleeping at the house but not always in her bed, drawing closer to Freida and getting to know Ivan, Christopher and Mr Harcourt a little better. He spent a lot of time with Ivan and liked him. Fergus appeared but remained much in the background. Jean had Freida get more keys cut so that each of them was able to come and go as they pleased. She sat in the garden and in the morning-room, eventually beginning her days upstairs in the formality of the Green Room, close to Aunt Dizzy's urn. Ivan loaned her some books on English history which she read, their dry factuality comforting. She did not listen to music, her own or anyone else's. The house stayed quiet, voices hushed not in a maudlin way but with a gentle quality of regret and sadness. Aunt Dizzy would have hated it, but for Jean it was part of a process of getting through to an acceptance that Elizabeth Doo Lally Barrie was no more to wander about in her hot pants or in almost nothing at all, leaving the odour of cigar smoke everywhere she went.

Each of them was dressed in their own version of finery by the time Father O'Connell arrived exactly on time. Jean had not wished to know much about him or his background beforehand, despite Freida's eagerness to tell all. He had, it seemed, quite a reputation in certain London circles and possessed numerous right-wing enemies as well as a legion of supportive friends. He was, surprisingly, quite small in stature, extremely polite and reticent, dressed in a quiet, formal grey flannel suit and sombre tie. Freida had asked for him not to be dressed in his usual garb of a cross between Catholic priest and Church of England bishop.

'He makes all his own frocks,' Freida announced in mock seriousness to a completely silent room before he appeared. Christopher sniggered.

Flowers had been set out in vases alongside the red carpet and inside the pink-and-white tent where the ceremony would take place. Father O'Connell went in for simplicity and brevity, the latter usually because he was in such great demand. Christopher went out with his father, followed closely by Fergus, stunning in a white suit, his face flushed and tinted monocle sparkling. Freida and Jean wore corsages; the men wore buttonholes of green carnations. There was no music and no delay and the entire blessing was over in fifteen minutes. Father O'Connell spoke beautifully in a modulated, calm and pleasant voice about tolerance and recognition of all the varied forms of commitment. Christopher and Fergus exchanged new, inscribed, solid gold rings and hugged. Mr Harcourt awkwardly read from a card for less than a minute about parenthood, the speech apparently provided by Father O'Connell. Freida smirked. Ivan Fitzpatrick seemed rather touched by the simple formalities and Jean was certain, when he glanced at her, that his eyes were moist. Christopher kept grinning, glancing over his shoulder at Jean. Somewhere outside the tiny tent, above them on a rooftop, could be heard for a moment the two collared doves that frequented the garden, giving out their own particular melody. As soon as the ceremony was concluded they withdrew back inside the house. The two hired cars Frieda and Ivan had arranged were already waiting out front, and within a very short space of time they were being driven off towards Soho.

It had been Freida who wished for the blessing to be conducted briefly and for the true celebration of the day to be held elsewhere at a restaurant. A last-minute decision, not discussed, it was made from respect for Aunt Dizzy's passing, which each of them was still recovering from and still so aware of, inside the house as well as in the garden.

•

Mrs Meiklejohn sat on a hard wooden chair in an inner windowless box room, dressed up to the nines, waiting for her own guests to arrive. She did not wish to be seen at the front of the house while all the dozens of Jean Barrie's guests would be arriving next door, along with, she had convinced herself and Nellie Harcourt, caterers and waitresses and all the implements of what she had decided was to be An Event at the Barrie residence. There had been many of those in the past, with all the trimmings. An entire brass band once. Noise and shouting and singing and drinking on the lawn, music never ending, all night, on so many occasions. Mrs Meiklejohn never once invited over, never forewarned, never apologized to afterwards.

As she waited she envisaged marching out into her garden with the others from the church at the appointed time, singing hymns, waving the placards: SODOMY WILL BRING DOWN THE WRATH OF JESUS. THE SINS OF THE FATHER WILL DESCEND ON TO THE SON. WICKEDNESS WILL BE PUNISHED. EVIL SOULS SHALL BE BANISHED TO HELL. The wording of the placards, the banners, was perfect if somewhat severe, she thought. She hoped there would not be trouble; Mrs Harcourt did not want authorities involved. Naturally she would be remaining indoors unseen, having pre-directed the action and written the slogans. Mrs Meiklejohn glanced at her wristwatch. It was noon. Her guests were late. She was tempted to take a peek out through the kitchen window but resisted. She might be seen. She was already trembling. She picked at red flakes of paint on the backs of her hands with her peach-varnished fingernails. She could hear nothing, of course, from next door, as the walls of her house were solid and insulated. She sat imagining the crowd arriving next door, as they had in the past, ready to party, ready to witness the execrable ceremony between Nellie's son and her evil brother. She grew angry then calm, anxious then resigned. She waited silently there in the inner room amongst cardboard boxes of abandoned magazines and books and the detritus of all the years.

'That was *it*?' Freida whispered to Jean as soon as the hired cars were driving away from the house, turning left at the top of Acacia Road. As they'd got into their car Freida had complained that the driver looked as if he had just been released from a high-security prison.

'You organized it,' Jean responded.

'It was far too short, Lady. Tutu short.'

'They loved it. Look at them,' Jean whispered back, gesturing up front. Fergus and Christopher, separated from the driver by a smoked-glass window, were gazing into each other's eyes in rapture, both smiling broadly, Fergus's arm around Christopher's shoulder.

'If you say so. It didn't really mean anything. Not really. Fred the Frock isn't even a real priest.'

'What is *wrong* with you? I found the service most touching.'

'Yes, lollypop, if you didn't *blink* ! That tent cost the earth to hire. Fred the Frock charged me a fortune – *in advance*. It was a rip-off. I'll have words.'

Jean glanced behind out the rear window. The other car was following closely. Ivan sat up front with the driver. He waved, and Jean smiled. Freida sat fuming, tapping her enormously long and immaculate nails on her knees.

Mrs Meiklejohn kept glancing at her watch. It was almost twelve thirty. The doorbell remained silent.

Freida, unbeknown to Jean, had booked the entire restaurant. She had peopled it with, to her mind, carefully chosen guests and friends, male and female, all of whom knew who Jean was and some who were fans. The restaurant was decked out in pink shades and streamers and giant cloth flags. There was to be a small orchestra under instruction to play only music from the 1920s and 1930s, a period Jean adored. Christopher and Fergus were to sit at their own table in front of the orchestra, on it a three-tiered wedding cake and, above, a pink-blossom-covered arbour. Amongst those present would be a scattering of drag queens and a group of female wrestlers, who were to give a demonstration of their talents to the music of Cher. Cedric Hyde was invited, numerous gay male friends and a dozen elderly men and women who were there to pay tribute to Aunt Dizzy, members of a social club – who went dancing and drank and smoked and still did aerobics – to which Aunt Dizzy had once belonged.

Just as the sound of Mrs Meiklejohn's doorbell reached her straining ears, the cars arrived outside the restaurant in Soho, and Freida, taking over, gathered everyone together on the pavement.

Nellie Harcourt stood at the door when Mrs Meiklejohn answered the bell.

'I have been ringing your bell for three minutes! No one is there!' Mrs Harcourt immediately complained. 'Next door! The house looks deserted. Are you sure you got the correct day, Alvina?'

It was, by then, gone one o'clock.

Mrs Harcourt had brought eight other women from the church, more than Mrs Meiklejohn thought she was to accommodate. Her first panicked thought, as she glanced at them over Nellie's shoulder, was whether or not she had made enough sandwiches. She had certainly made a mistake about what she wore. Each of her guests wore black severely cut two-piece suits with pleated skirts. Mrs Meiklejohn was dressed in an an elegant full-length fake-silk peach dress and she had spent hours on her hair, suffocating it with half a can of lacquer. The other ladies all wore black berets. In twos, the members of Nellie Harcourt's church filed sombrely into the hall, peering about them with superficially friendly stares, reading the placards, considering the mock-antique telephone, the flock wallpaper, paintings on the wall. Mrs Meiklejohn excused herself after showing them into the best room and hurried through into the kitchen, peering out the windows. Seeing no one across the wall, she quietly opened the door, fully irritated by the babble of voices now wafting out from her downstairs living-room.

Jean Barrie's garden was empty. Mrs Meiklejohn hurried down the path and stared through the gap in the wall. A vase of flowers had been overturned beside a red stretch of carpet. One green carnation lay on the grass. A black cat stood staring up at her; it mewed. Beside the closed french windows stood half a bottle of Tanqueray. As she lingered, not having noticed that the day had grown progressively grey as she had been hidden in the inner room, it began to rain. A light shower fell at first, then suddenly stopped. When a sudden, heavy deluge fell, Mrs Meiklejohn, still not having noticed the sky and intent on trying to peer through Jean Barrie's french windows into an empty room, let out a shriek.

'Fooled you, Lady,' Freida said as she ushered Jean, Christopher and Fergus through the doors into the restaurant. The others followed. Freida had been glaring at Fred O'Connell and had half playfully slapped his wrist. Immediately they entered there came a burst of loud applause and the orchestra began to play 'Mr Bojangles'.

'I was pretending, lollypop. About being miffed. It has *all* been engineered. Let the fun begin! Come on, I want to dance with you, whether you want me to or not. The whole place is *ours*!'

'You trollop!' said Jean, and held out her arms.

Jean danced with Freida. She danced with Christopher. She kissed Christopher twice and he kissed her back with moist rubbery lips. She danced with Fergus to a requested Viennese waltz, and then with Mr Harcourt. Cedric Hyde danced with Christopher. Christopher danced with anyone who asked. The women wrestlers wrestled to the music of Cher. Father O'Connell spoke at great length about love. Fergus spoke about himself and invited everyone there present to his country seat in Cheshire. Christopher wept. The group of elderly ladies and gents danced enthusiastically with each other and smiled vaguely with perfect dentures. Food was served. The tiered cake was cut. Champagne was sipped and spilt. Ivan stood up and sang an Irish ditty after drinking too much wine. Anthony arrived eventually and Jean danced with him and held on to his hand. Freida insisted on dancing with both of them.

'We've only got the place for two hours!' she shouted, throwing her arms around them. Anthony asked Jean to marry him, and she declined. She was asked to sing and said no to that. Everyone sang 'Happy Birthday' as she stood with her arms around Christopher and Fergus being photographed, laughing while Fergus whinnied.

She was to remember this day for a long, long time. She was to forgive Aunt Dizzy for leaving her. And while dozens of pink balloons floated down on to them from a suspended net and her friends, one after the other, each kissed her, she realized for the first time that she would have to make every effort in the years ahead also to forgive herself.